CRITICAL ACCLAIM FOR AWARD-WINNING

HANNAH'S HOUSE

AND AUTHOR
SHELBY HEARON

❧

"Everything comes together on Hannah's wedding day in a white gown ceremony complete with blue garter, bridal bouquet, old scores, false fronts and real tears."
—*New York Times Book Review*

❧

"A moving and effectively told story of one set of relationships between mothers and daughters, fathers and daughters, sisters, and all the tangled tissues of family.... If this is a novel for mothers and daughters to read, it is also very much a novel for fathers and sons to read."
—*Dallas News*

❧

"Hearon writes like a female Larry McMurtry, with humor, pain, surprise, and resolution in a single entertaining package."
—*Los Angeles Times*

more . . .

"Beverly is a very funny lady—sharp-witted, sensitive, occasionally incisive—who spins a sprightly and amusing tale about the year before her daughter's marriage. . . . The book is told in Beverly's voice, and it's an engaging one."
—*Houston Chronicle*

"She is the kind of novelist whose antennae of perception and nuances of insights would send any professional psychologist back to school to learn another trade. With the lightest touch imaginable she turns a character inside out, so that thoughts and feelings fall out as naturally as pollen in the wind."
—Evelyn Oppenheimer, National Public Radio

"Her writing gleams with the kind of labor and craft that comes from doing it the old-fashioned way."
—*Austin American-Statesman*

"For over two decades, Hearon has been writing beautifully made, extremely readable novels."
—*Village Voice Literary Supplement*

"Her writing is tight and clean and her craft so unobtrusive we hardly know it's there. Hearon sets up a scene or builds a character as quietly as a weaving spider—a tightly drawn line here, a connecting thread there. Then light falls on the web and the whole pattern is revealed in its beauty and intricacy."
—*San Francisco Chronicle*

"Hearon has a fine sense of place and
a sharp ear for dialogue."
—*People*
❧

"(Beverly's) thoughtful awareness of the public
and private sides of her life adds dimensions to
this introspective novel of relationships."
—*School Library Journal*
❧

"Hearon creates Southern women characters who
are wonderfully—and sometimes wickedly—
true to life."
—*USA Today*

A NOTE ABOUT THE AUTHOR

Shelby Hearon was born in Marion, Kentucky. She grew up in Kentucky but later moved to Texas, where she was graduated from the University of Texas at Austin. Over the years she has taught at a number of universities, including American Studies at the University of Texas at Austin, and creative writing at the University of Houston, Bennington College, and the University of California at Irvine. She was the recipient of an Ingram Merrill grant in 1987, a National Endowment for the Arts Creative Writing Fellowship in 1983, the John Simon Guggenheim Memorial Fellowship for Fiction in 1982, has five times won the NEA/PEN Syndication Short Story Prize, twice won the Texas Institute of Letters best novel award and won the literature award from the American Academy and Institute of Arts and Letters. Her next novel, Hug Dancing, *will be published in hardcover in the fall of 1991. She and her husband, Bill Lucas, live in Westchester County, New York. She has a grown daughter and son.*

BOOKS BY SHELBY HEARON

Owning Jolene   1988
Five Hundred Scorpions   1987
A Small Town   1985
Group Therapy   1984
Afternoon of a Faun   1983
Painted Dresses   1981
Barbara Jordan: A Self-Portrait   1979
(with Barbara Jordan)
A Prince of a Fellow   1978
Now and Another Time   1976
Hannah's House   1975
The Second Dune   1973
Armadillo in the Grass   1968

SHELBY HEARON

HANNAH'S HOUSE

WARNER BOOKS

A Time Warner Company

to my sisters
Frances, Susan and Linda
who are myself,
and to Evelyn and Charles
who began us.

Originally published in hardcover by Doubleday & Company, Inc.

Everyone in the book is fictional except the attorney who does live here in Austin and who did argue and win the Texas abortion case before the U.S. Supreme Court. However, the party she attends is fictional and she is never mentioned by name.

Warner Books Edition

This Warner Books edition is published by arrangement with
Doubleday & Company, Inc.
Garden City, New York

Warner Books, Inc., 666 Fifth Avenue, New York, NY 10103
 A Time Warner Company

Printed in the United States of America
First Trade Printing: September 1991
10 9 8 7 6 5 4 3 2 1
Library of Congress Cataloging in Publication Data

Hearon, Shelby, 1931-
    Hannah's house / by Shelby Hearon. — Warner Books ed.
        p.   cm.
    ISBN 0-446-39285-5
    I. Title.
PS3558.E256H3   1991
813' .54—dc20
                                                                91-18203
                                                                CIP

Cover design by Mario Pulice
Cover illustration by Joanie Schwartz

"Perhaps a bird was singing and for it I felt a tiny affection, the same size as the bird."

JORGE LUIS BORGES

Contents

Prologue

If I tell you that Mildred, my eldest sister, is married to an eldest brother, and that they are achievers, and that Dorothy, my youngest sister, is the baby of the family and married to a man who wants to keep her that way, and that I am the middle child of the same sex, you must not, in your social-scientist way, make judgments about us and miss the story I am telling. You only do that because putting us into categories and groups makes relating to a whole world of individuals possible.

Also do not draw conclusions based on what ninety-five per cent of persons who hate their names reveal. I am not ninety-five per cent of anything. Besides, I have good reasons: Beverly is a name that meant all that my parents expected of me at the same time that they made clear that I could never live up to it. Like any menial, I called myself by my last name. Foster, I told myself, you are all right in your place. Where is your place? For years in school while I was working on a long secret autobiography indicting my parents, I signed my name Bananas Foster instead of Beverly Foster at the top of my homework and on the title pages of my themes. I still send Christmas cards to Miss Fordyce, the only teacher who noticed this levity and kept me in after school. My life story was divided into three parts: the first was "The Making of Bananas Foster, By Which I Mean the Beginning"; the second was "The Making of Bananas Foster, By Which I Mean the Laying"; and the third was "The Making of Bananas Foster, By Which I Mean the Completing."

My problem then as now was my addiction to people. You will realize that addicted to does not mean affection for or delight in; it means you cannot help it. There are too many of us and we all have such entangled lives. We are at the same time constituted of large parts of the people who began us and who tug and pull to continue us, and smaller fragments of the hundreds of others at back-to-school night, traffic jams, the grocery store, the beauty shop, bus-station rest rooms. (All over the world at this instant millions of us are beginning.)

This is the story of how well I have or have not learned to handle such relating.

I wanted to name the chapters "Winter," "Spring," and

"Fall" to enable you to picture a scene change in which flats with painted leaves are lowered, alternating bare limbs with reds and golds and bushy greens, or, better yet, to name them "The Gazebo on a Summer's Night" and "The Gazebo Two Hours Later," but sequences did not arrange themselves this way. So, if the headings seem as unrelated as oranges and pigs, so do the vital episodes of our lives.

One: Hannah

1. Her House

Hannah tells the realtor that she loves the yellow stucco house. It is on a nice street, in a nice part of town. Bebe Lee, who was a cheerleader in high school, lives around the corner. The spectacular living room, its twelve-foot ceiling bordered with hand-glazed Mexican tiles of a quality to rival the excavations at Pompeii, would be a lovely place to entertain Hannah's friends. It is a house that she would be proud to be married from.

Poking into closets and corners, I deduce that it is on the market not only because there is a visible crack the height of the house on the plastered outside wall to the west, but also because its occupant has recently died. In a downstairs room that must have been a library, as it has floor-to-ceiling bookcases, is a hospital bed whose sheets have corners mitered as tightly as if a nurse had just left. A bedpan is on the closet floor; the adjoining bath has an enema bag on a hook behind the door; a wheelchair is folded in the ample pantry; a commode chair is in the back hall, covered with a sheet. The smell of the library, closed-up, disinfected, reminds me of old people's illnesses in my past, of my grandmother's house, of stories that my uncle the pharmacist was ever-ready to repeat.

"I see the owner has moved on," I tell our realtor.

She brushes this aside. "This isn't even on the market yet. You're the first people I've shown it to. It's definitely going in a hurry."

On a roll-top desk is a sheaf of prescriptions: in January the patient could add one number five Empirin every four hours as needed for pain. By March the dosage was increased to two number eight Empirin every two hours. By June the notes stop. Hospital time. Now, in August, nothing more is needed.

"Mother, don't you love it?" Hannah presses me for approval, for permission.

"Does the hospital bed come with it?"

"Mother, *please*—" She does not want to be embarrassed by her mother, not again, not this time. "Bebe Lee lives just around the corner," she pleads.

I mention the crack to drive down the price.

The realtor concedes, sees that she has made her sale. "You've really got a steal here. At this price I could sell it five times over. In this neighborhood I could sell a one-room shack. They'll clear out this stuff for you. The drapes stay."

Hannah glows. She has waited all her life for this house. Her dream is to have this address when her friends get back in town for rush week, and when Eugene gets back from the coast as her official fiancé. They could have the announcement party here, in this fine room with its winding stair and tiled fireplace flanked by arched niches like church altars.

"We're not buying a house," I observe, "we're buying a living room."

"Will it take long?" Hannah asks the realtor.

Our saleswoman assures her that certain procedures can be waived. That haste can be made. "If you'll just come on by my office, Beverly." The deal consummated, we are on a first-name basis.

For my daughter I answer to this name, for her I promise this woman a down payment equal to the sum of money which was set aside for Hannah's education and which will not be needed now that she is to be an Easter bride. My younger sister Dorothy was such a sophomore with white straight legs like asparagus stalks when she quit school to marry Charlie.

This Spanish-style house with its startling giant yucca plants along an old gravel driveway will make some changes in my life. The house where we are now, which has been the backdrop for my years with Ben, and Hannah's years as a member of the second-best crowd in junior high and high school and a member of a good sorority on campus, is not a show place. Its street is run down, its school-district boundaries have been redrawn, old shaggy trees bend out over the sidewalks. (It reminds me of streets in Sally, Texas, where I come from, where each yard, in my memory, has a mesquite tree to knock off the sun and each house has a washing machine on the back porch.) The house itself is shabby, although Hannah has had a way of making it look cluttered on purpose. She knows how to fill the bathtub with ice and Dr. Peppers and put out trays of Fritos and onion dip, for the slumber parties of her crowd or her pledge class.

Where we are now would have lasted me just fine. Shabby does not bother me. Genteel, shabby, not what we once were, are familiar stories from my childhood. Living on that street has been like living with a grandmother; like all old people, it has seen better days.

Where we are now has a kitchen table, that essential requirement for a home, that place to sit and read the paper and do most of the talking that matters. It also has a back bedroom off a screened porch with its own door where Ben lets himself in at night. I will miss the good sound of the creaking door, which can wake me from the soundest sleep.

Shabby is not a word Hannah can live with, and she made it through high school and rush in our comfortable old house because it was so convenient to school and because her best friend Jenny Sue lived two blocks over and because we hadn't known about the redistricting when we bought it. But it is not a place for her to leave home from; most of all it is not a place for Eugene's mother to come calling.

This yellow stucco house is to be the final gift to this daughter whose rearing has been my primary concern for nearly half my life. My work has not been in vain; she is what I never was: a friendly, steadfast girl who fits in where she should, who knows where she belongs. Even her name is constant: *Hannah spelled backward is Hannah.*

The realtor having put on fresh lipstick and gone off to gather together titles and dotted lines, we take a final walk around our new home. Hannah wears a shy, happy face; she redecorates and cleans and prepares this home in her mind to open it to those she loves.

The bedrooms are upstairs, one fair-sized one with a sunlit corner for plants and a small iron-railed balcony, one smaller one without a window. They share a white tiled bath with an antique tub. This upstairs will be all for Hannah. The little room can be her sewing room; she will like a whole room to spread out her patterns and yard goods. Like her aunts, Hannah makes her own clothes. Like them she shows by this that she can gauge to the very inch the size and shape of her own body. (One reason I have never sewn.)

Downstairs the dining room is on the back side of the house, a strong servant's distance from the cramped kitchen which, as the pantry and back hall were carved out of it, does not have room for a table.

The library off the living room will have to be my room; Ben will have to learn to come in the front door. It has its own bath and that fine wall of shelves, generous enough for both of us to put his books, if, in time, he does come to live with me. But his divorce is not the matter on my mind this fall; this fall is Hannah's. My future room has one very high window like those found in basements that makes the room seem below ground, though it is not, and makes me think you might look up to see the ankles of the yard man going by. This narrow rectangular space will make a satisfactory place for me: like a cat I like to feel my back safely to the wall.

In a week's time we have moved into the stucco house. Outside we have raked the gravel drive and hosed down the Mexican clay tiled roof until it shines like bricks fired in the sun. By the front door, for company to see, we have put three potted red geraniums which, so strongly is Hannah's longing for *niceness* conveyed to them, have flowered in the heat.

In the living room we have placed our good couch and chair around a secondhand rug that Hannah found. Its earth colors and hand-woven design look Navaho and do fine things for the dark floors and washed white walls.

Upstairs Hannah's things are arranged in order in her pink bedroom with matching curtains and dust ruffle, made by her, and in the small sewing room where she has her reconditioned Singer machine and a file box of patterns.

My room feels private, not a place that Hannah's friends would happen into. The rollaway bed from the shabby house is set under the high window like a window seat. At the other, darker, end of the long room is the desk which belonged to the former owner; it and its swivel chair were negotiated for as the hospital bed was being removed. The bookshelves have a surplus of books on overpopulation, from my office, a few Spanish writers in paperback that Ben has given me, and piles of old magazines. It, the room, has the mixed flavor of an undergraduate reading room and a Pullman berth. Very pleasant. Miss Fordyce, my sixth-grade teacher, or Ms. Fordyce as she would be now, would feel at home here. It looks as if the occupant understood what is important.

Lying in my bed in the morning I can hear the sounds of Hannah run down the water pipes and know that it is time to rise. She pees, she flushes, she brushes teeth, sudses face, rinses. The noise of her clawfooted bathtub draining is a summer downpour. The warm water pipes at the foot of my rollaway remind me of hotel rooms, as the bed itself reminds me of trains in the days of trains. Both create a fine lack of permanence to wake to.

Exposed water pipes and radiators remind me of places where you pay to sleep, because we did not have them at home. In some hotel room in Corpus, while Mildred and Dorothy slept, nice girls in pajamas with their heads on pillows, I crept up in the middle of the night to feel the two hot poles that ran up beside the window. It was comforting, like patting a dog in the dark. Three stories below, seen through dusty gauzy curtains, late cars moved on the streets, proving there were other people in the world besides Mildred and Dorothy.

Once in a motel room where I stayed briefly with Hannah's father (a Certified Public Asshole of whom more later, perhaps a minor footnote) I spent most of the night, while he snored, warming my backside against a hot radiator, wishing I were some other place with someone else. In Budapest or Dallas.

In Sally, Texas, we had no radiators; they were considered out of date, like Venetian blinds. We had a floor grill where you could stand to let hot air blow up your skirt for the few scattered weeks of winter. We had no rollaway beds or secondhand desks; each piece of our heavy furniture had sat in its designated place so long it seemed to root us for life to where we had always lived.

A nice contrast that this room, if not the house it adjoins, feels like a place you could leave at any time.

Roy drops by for lunch to case the new higher-rent location. He is good to have around; he waits on himself and is easy to talk to. Hannah's old boy friends usually move on when she is through with them, but Roy, who worked as a mechanic in high school and is now going to night school at the community college and working full time at a garage, still comes by. Halfway, I think, to get news of Hannah, halfway because I don't hassle him like his mother does.

When I don't eat with Ben in the faculty dining room or get a quick lunch up the street with my supervisor, I usually end up at home having a peanut butter sandwich. When I do, it is often shared with Roy, who today roared down our new driveway scattering gravel with the same style that he used to burn rubber on the asphalt at the old house.

Today we have pulled straight chairs up to the kitchen window and set our iced tea glasses on the sill as if we were at some country farmhouse. The window—its screen propped open with a stick—is a focal point to sit around. It furnishes a constant view much like sitting before an open fire; we see an old stone fountain, dry, and an unfenced yard of browned grass. The sun comes in through the open window to make a light streak on the faded vinyl asbestos floor that was originally patterned to look like cobblestones.

Roy says, "There'd be room for a table here if that swinging door wasn't there. Why don't you unhinge it?"

"Hannah doesn't want my sink exposed to the world."

"She doesn't want Eu-gene to see what a dump you keep."

"Something like that."

After a minute: "I could build a shelf. See?" He demonstrates a collapsible table top, like one of those ironing boards that fold out from a cabinet in the wall, that would lie flat across the wall below the window and raise up into a table when we're sitting. We imagine it together; I see myself eating my doughnut and reading the morning paper as Hannah has her diet cereal.

"That would be great."

"You'd have to pay me for the lumber."

"Sure." I finish my tea, visualizing my table. "If you want to help, come look at this garbage mess."

I show him the pantry which is now full, waist high, of green plastic bags with twisted wires around their throats. The small niche looks and smells like the concealed remains of an abattoir. At the old house I put my garbage out at night, and, even if the can was dumped over by dogs, Willard, my garbage man, would pick it up and leave a bare clean spot in the alley. Here, in this nice neighborhood, we have to set the cans out on the street in front of the lawn and on Monday they were overturned and scattered down the street—a mess of coffee grounds, cans, eggshells, used Kotex, dripping ice cream cartons. The Sanitation Supervisors in their afros, muscle shirts, and hip boots riding by on their truck did not pick up anything that was not enbagged. They did not pick up anything and they conveyed that they did not want the chocolate cake I used to give Willard every Christmas, that, in fact, anything I could offer, they did not want. So Thursday at six in the morning in my old robe I carried out the trash which I had kept for days in my pantry, and weighted the can lids down with rocks.

Roy says, "You ought to get buried cans."

"Are you volunteering to dig me some?"

"I could build you a three-sided fence around one of those trees out front and you could set the cans out of sight. You know, plant ivy or some stuff. You'd have to pay me for the lumber."

"Hannah would be relieved."

"Lumber's cheap."

We close the pantry and he tours the living room. "She must be proud of this dump."

"She is. She even has a room upstairs for her sewing machine."

"Yeah. Lots of new rags for the fi-ancé, I guess."

"My sister sent her some material for a long dress."

"If she didn't have those society types behind her pushing all the time—" He is too slight to be the movie hero who knocks all the dishes off the table or the perfume bottles off the dresser, and, besides, he isn't that good-looking. But he walks in a way that qualifies him: very slow with all the muscles in his legs moving, which is very effective in his tight jeans with their suitable bulge and his T shirt that shows his rib cage. If you were a girl and he began to mess with you it should be very pleasant. But he is not someone Hannah could accept; his family is not much and his reputation is no better.

"See you around," he says. "You got to get back to sterilizing the goons."

"We can't all grease cars." We smile good-by.

He takes my job at HEXPOP personally, as if all talk of overpopulation meant his family wasn't wanted around here, as if this world wouldn't want his kids.

Hannah, scrubbed and brushed, asks, "Does this look all right?" She shows me her blouse which is skybaby blue and its matching skirt which falls to her white ankles. Mildred has matched her niece's eyes with yards of flowered cotton.

"It's lovely, honey."

"My hair is clean, anyway." With pride she smooths her thick mass of flaxen hair. She has a way of patting it on each side of her cheeks that she has had since she was a little girl. A gesture that provides her with the comfort she longs for.

"It looks lovely."

We are in the fine living room, where evening light coming through the vaulted windows illuminates the tiled frieze like a flashlight in a ruin. We are waiting for Eugene, who has not seen the yellow stucco house. He asked for her hand on his birthday, to keep her his while he went with his mother for their annual three weeks to the coast. Next year, he promised Hannah, he would be taking a wife with him.

My shirtwaist dress is rumpled from work; I am not the compleat mother of a sophomore, but Eugene will sooner or later have to deal with my reality, although, for Hannah's sake, I will try to make it later.

"Mother?" Shyly she brings up a question. "D-do you think Ben will have his divorce in time to give me away? I mean if you think he'd like to do that and all. I could ask Uncle Charlie or Uncle Dick if you'd rather. If you think Granddaddy for sure can't travel because of his back. I mean, I don't want to rush you all or anything."

Hannah stammers slightly over matters of grave importance, which helps me sort such occurrences from the usual in her life, as all her concerns appear to me uniform, linear, and solvable, so solidly is she set in her own sphere.

A blush appeared on her face at the effort of asking this question; she has never quite managed to live with the fact that I am not married to Ben. She is so vulnerable to that which is ordinary that I have to look away to answer.

"He plans to file this month. He has waited out seven years. But your guess is as good as mine how long it will take; these things take time."

"I was just asking."

"I'm sure he'd like to give you away. Ask him. Or do you mean you only want him to if we are married? Hannah, we can't both get married this spring; think of the florist's bill."

She looks hurt at this.

I try to be done with it. "You can ask Dick if it doesn't work out with Ben. He and Mildred considered you almost their own all the years they didn't have children." But not Charlie. Charlie is not about to give any child of mine away that he didn't want to be in on the beginning of.

"Mother," she hesitates, "you do love him, don't you?"

"Ben? Of course."

"I mean, it's hard to tell with grownups. You know, they don't act the same. You know what I'm trying to say, they act more like married people."

As opposed to people who love each other. Astute. And coming from a bride-to-be. "I understand."

Love, however, is not what Hannah thinks it is. Love is not who is your maid of honor or when you get your ring or how much his mother likes you. Love is that the person you are with is here with you and nowhere else, even in his mind. Which is one thing to consider about Ben; he may never be without the presence of his onetime pregnant wife.

Hannah wants to be able to tell Eugene and his mother, and Jenny Sue and the house mother, that her mother, a sort of widow, is going to marry an old friend of the family.

My mind observes that her version will be inaccurate: the CPA is alive and unpleasant in Arkansas with a second wife whom he deserves. A second wife who is, I trust, slovenly and shrewish.

"I didn't mean to pry or anything—"

This is a tiring discussion. How can I always be put in the position of declaring to her what may or may not be true. Ben, yes; marriage, why? But her longing insists upon reassurance. "Yes," I tell her. "Yes. After all, Foster and Roberts have the same vowels in the same order and three of the consonants repeat; because of these coincidences I will consider farding myself with still another last name whenever Ben can untie the knot."

"Oh, Mother." She turns to go, but then has to turn back and fetch forth a smile and bring herself to deal with me further. There is one more question. "Do you think I ought to ask D-Daddy?"

"To give you away?"

"Would he get his feelings hurt, do you think, if I didn't?"

Would he care if we were both run over by a train? "If you want him to, honey, I'll drive up to Arkansas and bring him back here myself. He owes me a few favors."

"I didn't really mean that, Mother. I was just wondering if I ought to invite him to the wedding and all. Maybe I'll just write him about it; he would want to know."

"Do that."

We are rescued by the doorbell.

It is Eugene, standing in the doorway of Hannah's house. "Good evening, Mrs. Landrum." He has a direct way of looking at me, of shaking my hand, as if he were determined to go through with this.

"Hello, Eugene. How was Port Aransas?"

"Fine."

Hannah looks up at him and they say hi and he squeezes her hand and blinks his eyes at her happy face, now as pink as her room upstairs.

"Let me show you the house," she says shyly. She leads him across the dark wood floor to admire the fireplace.

"If you're sure I'm not intruding." He looks at me.

"Not at all, Eugene. I'm going to take a shower. You all have a good time out tonight."

As I close my door he says, "I really like it, Hannah." As their footsteps go up the winding stair to look at her bedroom I imagine her cheeks blooming as red as bashful roses.

Ben likes the house also; it is not as threatening to him as the run-down place where we lived before, which was too reminiscent of houses he himself had lived in. Remembering that he once knew what full-bodied meant as it pertained to fermented grapes and imagining the twelve-foot living room as the future scene of faculty wine-tasting parties, he brought us tonight a bottle of Cabernet Sauvignon, domestic, which he pronounced very tasteful, meaning it in both senses of the word.

Since Hannah had promised to be late, we drank it in our underwear on the rollaway, and did not watch the clock as we made love.

Now we lie together, talking. Below us four bare legs stretch out on the bed; they are very poignant, as they are middle-aged, and pale from never getting in the sun, and hairy, his, and somewhat veined, mine. They are legs that could be anyone's: it is moving that they are ours.

There is as little place here to tell of Ben as there is time to see him. He is a man widening in the middle and thinning on the top and still mooning for a girl who gazes blankly into space and stuffs her mouth with food. That girl, his wife, is pregnant no longer, and hasn't been for many years, and is no longer free to sit on a bench beside him. In another few months when he has severed his ties with her, he intends to marry again, despite his past bad luck with it. I don't pursue it; marriage is not all it could be and I am most reluctant to repeat an act that gave me such a sickness. I have been vaccinated against it. But if one were going to undertake living with someone, Ben would be as good a man as any.

He and I met at back-to-school night when our girls were about eleven. The year his wife was going under, or in, or down and back—whatever you say to mean away from the world and into herself. "Hello, aren't you Hannah's mother?" "Yes, and you're Van's daddy?" "What do you think of the new teacher?" "Several things."

The next year we walked from assembly to our classroom together. "Hannah is a very talented girl." "Van's math is better than the boys', isn't it?"

We made it to junior high where our girls had the same classes for the last time. By junior high we had each figured out that there was no husband or wife to appear.

By the time Hannah was into home ec and on the pep squad and Van was already into accelerated algebra and fighting the administration for the right to take mechanical drawing, we relaxed enough to leave the school together. "If you think our girls can be left a while longer, would

31

you like to go with me to get some supper? Is there a place still open at nine o'clock? I had a seminar and never ate."

"Do you mean to feed me, too?"

"I have a grant."

"HEXPOP has one, too."

"Do I have to present my credentials? One child and a vasectomy."

"What a waste, my tubes are tied."

We were awkward; we didn't do well. We were, of course, ahead of the game; it was only suppertime, and we were clumsy in our effort to begin a courtship.

As we ate Ben said, "I don't even know your name."

I wanted to get what might be my only lasting affair of the heart off to a truthful start, so I said, "My real name is Hannah's mother."

Now, flat on his back, staring at the ceiling, Ben says, "I'm going up there Sunday."

"I know." I hate his trips to see Van, Sr. He comes back like a man waking from a bad dream. Sometimes he doesn't come to my bed for a week or more.

"I'm going to tell her. I have to if I'm going to file when I get back."

"That will be hard."

"Who knows? She never says anything anyway. She just looks, and rocks herself." He accepts it. "As Borges says: 'like all men I am given bad times in which to live.'"

We hold hands for a minute. His hand grips tight with fingers that are red and blunt. His hand mirrors his character.

"Hannah wants you to give her away," I tell him.

"To that mama's boy?"

"She wants a father."

"She's come to the wrong place." He thinks of Van, Jr., who is at Antioch, living with a painter. Living with a painter and not answering her father's letters. He does not understand his daughter, as she, unlike mine, has never been a part of a nubile, budding group of girls. Van, Jr., has always been just Van.

"How long do divorces take?" The answer might well be years.

"It ought to be routine. Ought to have plenty of time to rent a tux for father-of-the-bride."

"She has uncles."

"I'm better than uncles." He is buoyed by this incentive to get the thing over with. "Hand me my shirt. Do we have time for coffee?" He is reluctant to get dressed, but he accepts things the way they are. He lives with the facts. He sees himself after all as merely as substudy of a middle-class, balding male with a living to earn, a man therefore not to be judged too harshly. If he is given to mooning over certain girls in his anthropology classes, if he is prone to take a long time acting, he is, after all, only a part of his culture. Ben forgives himself his humanity.

It is true that marriage means we could roll over and go to sleep, could wake up for love and breakfast even with Hannah in the house. But I have reservations. It has never been proved that the institution itself doesn't change the people. Marriage may be so constituted that inevitably when he wants to make love you need to go to the bathroom, that when you criticize his attitudes he checks your monthly calendar. It may be constructed so that even Ben—his widening stance, his changeable wrinkled face—will grow sullen upon finding that it is tuna fish for supper again.

As we have coffee and expand into the rest of Hannah's house we talk about the usual things: his students, his projects, my job. He looks around and admires the living room which seems to him a justifiable reason for legalizing what has been a very fine thing.

2. Her Friends

This September evening is the annual mother-daughter tea that follows rush week and the pledge line at the sorority house. I am to attend in the dress Hannah bought me for this, last year, when she was a brand-new pledge. The dress is a long aqua acrylic with wrist-length sleeves, a mock turtle neck and a belt crusted with aqua beads. It was hard for me to understand, especially after looking at the price tag, why Hannah had not wanted to make her mother's dress; after all, she had made her dresses for rush and her own long pink formal for the tea.

"This isn't the kind of dress you can make, Mother. You see the way that it fits you shows it's ready-made and the way the belt is trimmed; I just can't copy that. I mean, you ought to have a dress like this anyway. And you can wear it next year, too. It won't go out of style."

It didn't seem to have any style to lose. There was a backless black skinny dress that I tried on without a bra to see how my hipbones and nipples looked, protruding through the undulating jersey. It had style; but Hannah looked as if she might cry when I modeled it before the three-way mirror.

The aqua has hung unworn in my closet for a year. But Hannah is right; it will come in handy. There will be parties, to announce and shower and rehearse her wedding. It is a dress that will do fine in the company of Eugene's mother.

This mother-daughter tea is one more ceremony in a long procession of functions at which Hannah has had to count on me to appear and to produce what other parents did. There were the nursery school pageants, Brownie scout craft shows, pep squad suppers, junior high ball games, carpools to dance class, slumber parties, the first frenetic boy-girl parties, the Singer Sewing class style shows. And more.

Hannah has always done at her age what other girls did at the same age. If there was a gang who met by a certain locker before school, then Hannah was by that locker. If there was a place that the boys went after school to have a cigarette but it was all right for nice girls to go, then Hannah piled in someone's car and went. Even Roy, back when he was one of the first boys to drive and one of the only ones who liked to dance, was all right to go out with if you didn't go too far with him.

Hannah and Jenny Sue have been best friends since the fifth grade, when their crowd was first starting to gather together. They were all a solid group by the time of junior high school cheerleader tryouts, for although these groups added and dropped members as new girls were looked over and as popularity soared and waned they each revolved around the one or two girls, the stars, who held them together. In Hannah's crowd Cheryl was the star.

She was the girl they had believed from grade school was destined to be head cheerleader and class favorite and Most Beautiful when her time came. She was the one they later nominated and made posters for and voted for all through high school. The crowd that theirs competed with, which was a faster group as far as car dates and smoking and the type of boys they went out with, orbited around Bebe Lee, a blonde who was elected head cheerleader as well as Most Friendly and Most Beautiful the year Cheryl was only the runner-up, More Beautiful. Jenny Sue and Hannah and their friends commiserated with Cheryl when she didn't win what she had always been led to believe she was meant to win; they said that plain and simple jealousy kept most girls from voting for her.

By their senior year the crowd was promising each other to stick together no matter what, even in college, even if they pledged different sororities. They were inseparable through the last dances they gave, the last all-night parties, the last Saturday lunches of hamburgers and

Dr. Peppers, the very last morning of school when they congregated in their special place in the long, peeling hall of the old high school.

But sororities break up these high school bonds. Once you pledge you give yourself to a higher loyalty. And therefore, when Bebe Lee was in Jenny Sue and Hannah's pledge class and was pushed by the chapter for Most Beautiful Freshman and won, Jenny Sue and Hannah handed out carnations for her on campus. Now lots of the old crowd say that Cheryl won't ever get anything like Sweetheart because she is too stuck on herself, but not Jenny Sue and Hannah, who are very fair and loyal.

The girls in both crowds were somewhat surprised when people they never even heard of pledged the best sororities, but in general they understood and accepted such matters as family connections. They lost track right after graduation of the girls who finished high school and went right to work. And they had never kept track of the girls who slipped off into good universities and colleges on the East Coast and West Coast. Girls like Van, Jr., who were not in a crowd. Like me, all she was in, in high school, was her classes.

Hannah was a favorite among the girls in her group because she was a friend who could be counted on to help roll your hair in those days or help you out when you were caught with a cigarette in the hall or help you decorate for a party with yards and yards of crepe-paper streamers and posters on the den wall held up with Scotch tape and yellow light bulbs screwed into all the lamps because pink light bulbs made your skin look washed out.

My clearest memory of them all is in the fall of their senior year. All of them were in the tight tops and short skirts of the pep squad, in boots with tassles, waving pompoms. They were in the yard of the captain of the football team, before the big game, stringing between two trees a twenty-foot-long banner that read: CRUCIFY CORPUS CHRISTI.

Hannah said to me as I let her in the car, "Mother, *please*. I don't know what's so funny about that. I mean, we're playing Corpus tonight."

Rush week itself was all it was supposed to be. And Hannah and Jenny Sue did what was expected of them: they ate their hearts out for one of the best groups, which did not ask them back; they threw all their friendly energies into a second-best, some of whose members remembered them from junior high. By the last parties they were certain of a bid from a third group who believed they were stealing the girls from their second choice. And by the week of registration they wore on their rounded bosoms the two-colored pledge ribbons of the group which was, by then, and will be always, for they are very loyal, their very first choice.

It must have been somewhat like that for Mildred and Dorothy who were both in sororities because of the influence of some cousins of ours in Corpus, daughters of my mother's sister, who married well. They both wrote letters for Hannah and arranged courtesy dates for her. Mildred, if memory serves, was pledge trainer for her group at the height of her career, and Mother, who lives our lives, bragged on this fact about her eldest daughter often. Dorothy, when she came along with her straight white teeth and smooth white shoulders, was rushed by almost everyone. Mother didn't have to tell me this, by then I was already at the university, watching Dorothy charm, welcoming her to stay with me until she got settled, introducing her to Charlie. Her group wanted her so badly they bumped a legacy to get her. Or so she told me, dismayed. Dorothy is very gentle and never means to take what doesn't belong to her. It is a gift she didn't seek that she has that softness that makes others gather to save her. Her even teeth like shoe-peg corn look prey to cavities, her creamy skin to melanoma, her straight white legs to varicosity. There was no way to blame Charlie.

Hannah was proud and grateful to have her aunts' recommendations for her and did her very best: she made new dresses for each round of parties, washed her cascade of hair every night, and didn't even break silence with Jenny Sue, although they both knew they would pledge the same thing if they could. And when she called her aunts to tell them, they were quite relieved; her group was as good as theirs and her mother had not handicapped her.

"This is the happiest day of my life," Hannah said to each in turn.

I come home for lunch to get a quick sandwich before going to get my hair done for the evening's event. Roy arrives soon after the peanut butter is out on the hinged white-pine shelf that he built, which, raised and propped, now serves us as a table top.

"You're in a hurry," he says, after helping himself to lunch and splitting between us a Lone Star beer that he brought.

"Going to get my hair fixed."

"Someone died?"

"Mother-daughter tea at the sorority house."

"No shit." He wipes his mouth on his sleeve and stares out the window at the deserted yard.

One thing about Roy I like is that he is content to sit in this square footage which he says is six feet by six feet. He does not have to be entertained in the room with a twelve-foot ceiling and a frieze of tile. He does not need china plates for his sandwich. This attitude to space makes sense to me as the time will come when there are so many of us that two people will learn to get along in an area like this. They can lower their table top flat under the window after supper and swing their bedmat down from the wall. There they will lie in the dark and drink their wine and talk awhile, as when four or six families are assigned to a house like this, there will be no lights to read by. They could do worse than have a space this pleasant with its open rectangle to the changing weather.

When I was in high school I would have given almost anything, if I had had almost anything to give, to have times like these when nobody wanted anything of me but to be there. Beverly Foster, then, spent a lot of time trying to figure out what it was that pleased her mother, and then, because one depended on the other, what it was that would get her in the middle of girls and looked at by boys. But all that never seemed to catch on for me in high school. It made more sense to sit and talk with Miss Fordyce about the books she kept in her desk drawer.

There must have been boys like Roy around who weren't ever going to leave Sally, Texas, who weren't going much of anywhere, but they were not looking for me; they were trying to feel up the cheerleaders, then as now. If they kept blankets in the trunks of their rebuilt cars, they didn't ask me to try them out.

I tell Roy, "The garbage men have been nicer since you built the fence for the cans. No surly sneers. No kicking the cans with their hip boots."

"Those studs got nothing better to do than kick cans."

"There's some German chocolate cake left."

"If I eat after Eu-gene I'll puke."

"You guessed it."

"Passed Hannah standing on campus by the fountain yesterday holding that fag's hand. Honked but she pretended not to hear me. She was looking up at him like he was seven feet tall. Where do chicks learn to look through their eyelashes like that?"

"In my day from the movies."

"Must be. Not from their folks. Mom only uses hers to squint at me and ask where do I think I've been."

"The trick doesn't stay with you."

"After you get him." He shows his disgust. "She'll serve that cake to him again if I don't eat it. Might as well be me."

"Help yourself."

"You on a diet?"

"No. But I had to sit in there last night and eat cake with a sterling silver fork and wipe my mouth with a monogrammed linen napkin. Once is enough."

He cuts himself some of the sticky caramel-coconut iced dessert, eating hunkered over the table like an early imitation of Brando in an undershirt.

Hannah, who watched Eugene cut his cake neatly with a fork as his mother had taught him, would be displeased to see Roy eating like this. Just as she registered a dismay almost verging on anger when she found out that he had been back around and, more than that, had interfered with her house by building me the sturdy pine shelf.

The reappearance and the unpainted board were, however, made bearable by his solution to the garbage problem, although she instructed me to pay him for the lumber and not let him back in the house again.

"How're your classes coming?"

"You're just like Mom." He shoves back his chair.

I put the cake up and rinse his plate, getting ready to go get waved. My kitchen smells of peanut butter; I meant to have a kitchen that smelled of ripening tomatoes and fresh herbs. Another of those things you mean to do and don't.

"The prof still hang around?"

I nod. "He may move in."

"Legal, you mean."

"Legal. Hannah would like a father."

"Sure. You need an old man for a big white virgin church wedding." He leans on the counter. "You want him to?"

"I think so."

"You'll be busy if he does."

"How do you mean?"

"His kind never does anything for himself. Got to be picked up after."

Roy has bad ideas of fathers, his own being long gone. Which does not preclude his observing the truth.

"Do you pick up after yourself?"

He shrugs. "When Mom hassles me."

"That's sort of how I remember marriage. Hassling."

43

"Yeah," he agrees. "Take it easy. Tell the princess I ate her sweet boy's cake."

At the beauty shop the hairdresser does all she can for me in an hour and a half. As she demonstrates her skill—flicking large pink rollers and smaller red ones into place with the staccato rhythm of a tap dancer—she brings me up to date on her life story.

The younger sister who was pregnant last time has married the boy though he is no account and already running around. Ginger's own husband is nagging her to lose weight but she thinks she'll work it off because she has enrolled in an Arthur Murray dance class and if all he wants to do is stay home and guzzle beer, well, the studio promises you partners.

Under the dryer as I dutifully study the beauty magazines, it is clear that I am in the wrong epoch. There must have been a time for dark circles and sallow skin with just the hint of consumption, a time for labor-leader eyebrows. I study a two-page spread on powdered blusher and a page of closeups on the new thinner, paler brows that harken back to Jean Harlow.

When she brings me back and combs me out I tell her. "That looks fine, Ginger."

"Some better. You ought to come in more often and let me give you a body wave and conditioner. You've got some terrible split ends. You can't take proper care of it if you only come in twice a year."

In the mirror there is a smooth motherly wave on each temple, and, in the hand mirror, a deep swirl in back. "When do you start at the dance studio?"

"I go three times a week to begin, that's part of the

introductory offer, and then I decide where I want to be placed and only go once a week. He may sit up and take notice if I'm gone three nights in a row, and he can put a tail on me if he wants, because it's all on the up and up and I'll be right there where I said I would."

"My sister Dorothy took dancing lessons once, in high school."

"I should of done that, but I was working."

"She's a good dancer."

"I'm not so bad myself."

I leave her a tip. Thinking on the fact that millions of us around the world means millions and millions of sagas such as the dance class and the beer-drinking husband and the pregnant sister. It is hard to conceive of so many individual lives.

When I get home from work Hannah tells me that some woman called for me. "She said, 'This is Clarice Watson and I tried to catch her at the office.' So I didn't ask her anything else. I thought it must be a friend of yours." Hannah looks expectant, pleased that a woman has called for her mother. It is a touch of normalcy she hungers after, that she, too, might have a mother with friends. She has the air of one who believes that, if you smile a lot and do your best, things will work out for you. Which proves that my child-rearing has not been without its falsehoods.

"Clarice called" reminds me—this entire scene in the dining room concerning this call reminds me—of the semester my mother waited for me at the door with unconcealed excitement in her voice. "Bev, a little friend named Judy called for you." She told my sisters proudly, "Beverly got a call from her friend Judy at school."

The only Judy in Sally, Texas, lived at the company town and would have no reason to call me. In all of school there was not one girl who could be calling me for any reason, not even to volunteer that she had found my test paper or my health book. These were turned in to Miss Fordyce. But by that time in my life I had matured enough to lie. Which I did. "She wants me to join Y-Teens with her, Mom." And I even went so far as to get money from my mother to join the Y-Teens, as she believed in those things you had to pay for.

Mother knew about the Y-Teens because the officers' pictures had been on the front page of the Sally *Sentinel*. Mom always read the *Sentinel*, as she was secretary-treasurer of the Ladies' Auxiliary to the Volunteer Fire Department, and had had her picture in the paper, which was very prestigious, for although Mrs. Payne was president, she was president of everything and that didn't count.

We continued like this, Mother and I, for several weeks, during which I elaborated on my friend and even went so far as to say things like, "If you give me a dollar, Mom, we might stop for a Dr. Pepper coming home, Judy and me." Or maybe in those days I only asked for a quarter. Judy made such an upswing in my relations at home that she got me graduated from high school in the good graces of my family.

When the real Judy finally caught me at home it was to explain that I had not paid my class dues and could not be in the yearbook until I had. A nice girl calling all the seniors because she was secretary of the class, which I had forgotten about. "That was just Judy, Mom; thanks for getting the phone. We were deciding what to wear tomorrow." And the petty cash money was dug out of its hiding place.

Clarice will be more of the same. In Hannah's house am I allowed to tell the truth? "I don't know anyone named Clarice."

"Oh, but she sounded like you did, Mother. Like you'd know who she was—" Begging me.

History repeats. "She must be the new staff person down the hall, at the family service agency. I promised her we'd get together for lunch sometime. But I'd forgotten her name."

"That's great, Mother. You really need someone like that. I mean, you need to get out with your own friends. Gosh, I couldn't get along without Jenny Sue with all the studying and extracurricular stuff they want us to do at the house."

"Hmmmmmmm." My hair is waved, and there is Boston lettuce to make a salad. We have two veal cutlets to fry before we get into our party clothes.

Hannah and Jenny Sue will, in due time, be diapering their first children and getting together with Cheryl and Bebe Lee for sewing club, and working in the Symphony League for the girls who are now the pledge trainer and song leader of the chapter. They will move right along into new groups very like, slightly shifted from, the old groups. Other girls will become the stars to help them feel a part of one another, secure that they belong together, are somehow set apart from the girls who are not included. But I feel, as I did in high school, as Van Jr., must have, that the only thing harder to understand than being on the outside is being on the inside.

I'm never going to be able to give Hannah a view of women's friendship that she will identify with. Considering the cutlets, I decide, not for the first time, that if you are to give your best efforts to make a normal daughter, you must be willing to be judged by the sharp and limiting edges of normalcy.

Hannah likes to eat in the dining room, an airy room on the other side of the swinging door from my shelf, whose three large bay windows are sashed with starched white curtains. Starched by Hannah.

"Pass the salt, please." She tries out her manners. She cuts her meat, wipes her mouth with her napkin, finally balances her fork and knife on the edge of her plate to indicate she has finished. She demonstrates a charm course in eating, in preparation for Eugene's mother who has started including her for Sunday night supper.

It makes me tired, the vast energy of her will to please. The cutlet is dry, the salad has too much vinegar. Clearly I am not ready to take a husband again.

"Eugene," Hannah tells me proudly, "says he never knew a girl before who hadn't tried pot."

"It's like finding a virgin?"

She takes me seriously, as she always does. "Don't you think the two sort of go together?" She blushes. "Of course we don't talk about anything like that, but Eugene *knows*—I mean, he can tell that I've never let anyone take advantage of me."

"Roy came by today," I change the subject, mildly aware of my train of thought.

"You shouldn't let him, Mother, you promised last time. He really is a no-good person: I know from experience. Just tell him I'm not here and make him leave."

"He ate a piece of the German chocolate cake."

She draws herself up, injured. "If Eugene knew he was hanging around after me again he'd tell him off. I know he would."

We clear the table. Hannah stacks the dishes neatly for me to wash. "Mom? If you don't mind my asking, doesn't it bother Ben for Roy to come around when you're here? I mean, you and he are going to get married and all."

"He has students around all the time. He knows about strays like Roy."

"I was just asking. Because, well, you and Ben are going to get *married*." As she leaves to get ready she reaches up to pat her flocculent hair for comfort. Her mother makes her uneasy.

Ben comes to see us off, amused at me girdled and beaded with a forehead ruddy from blusher, brows newly plucked. As he pats my behind through the thick gathers, Hannah appears before us in a flowing ivory gown that falls to the floor like a length of marble. She is all that I have given myself to make: sensible, lovely, embarrassed to see her mother's backside fondled.

As we leave, Ben gives her a kiss, somewhat in the manner of an uncle. Shyly, Hannah offers him her soft daughterly cheek. "Doesn't Mother look nice?" she asks.

"She looks the part, anyway."

"Well." She doesn't want to rush him. "We'll see you after while?"

"Not tonight. Got a seminar at eight. We'll be there half the night." As he puts us in the car he kneads my hand in what seems to be a promise that he will join me much later in bed.

From Hannah he gets all the details about the tea and goes off cheered by the predictable pattern of this fine tribal rite.

"You look just great, Mother. That dress is just perfect." Hannah drives us slowly and carefully in the right lane of traffic. "Don't forget when I introduce you that Mrs. Archer is the housemother, and of course you remember Mrs. Garner is Jenny Sue's mother."

"Mrs. Archer and Mrs. Garner. I have it."

She stops our clean, vacuumed, very used Plymouth in an assigned parking slot. From other cars around us girls pour onto the lawn of the elegant formal house. They all look like Hannah: full of confidence and diffidence at the same time. They look, in their long dresses, as if none of them had been a cheerleader but that each of them had lived around the corner from one. They wave and call to each other and remind their mothers who everyone is.

Hannah is nervous. Whether because I am with her, although we did this last year, or because it all matters so very much, is not clear. Her trusting face is rosy, madeup, and smiling, but her hand, when she gives mine a squeeze, is damp.

I try to imagine myself in her place, their places, but am unable to do so. At that time in my life, as now, I could never have reached out for that massive, brass-knockered door without wondering what I was doing there, and, finding no answer, leaving.

"Don't you want to even go through rush?" Mildred had asked when I got to the university. Although graduating and engaged she took it upon herself to be responsible for me: she gave me a new lipstick and an almost-new cashmere sweater with only a small hole under the arm. Strange as I was, in an old shirt of Dad's and blue jeans a generation ahead of my time, she was willing to make an effort for me. It was her duty as the eldest. But it was with mutual relief that we hit upon the idea that I was probably transferring out of state after a semester or two.

But I did neither: I didn't pledge and I didn't transfer. At the university there were several courses far better than Miss Fordyce's. And there was, finally, after Charlie moved on, the CPA with his ingratiating ways. Things could not have been set with the right priorities in my years in college if the only choices I found were between a clique of girls and the start of a bad marriage. There must have been other Beverlys around from small towns like Sally and Dimple and Starr and Bug Tussle with glasses sliding down their noses in the Texas heat, who were changing their names to Foster. What a shame we did not find one another.

It was similar to high school where the groups of those who are out are just as excluding as those who are in and there is little place for those of us who need to deal one by one. The problem for me of sorting out an individual or two is worse now as at HEXPOP we deal with four and a half billion others grouped into crowds so vast as to be called by names such as Chinese, Arabs, Vietnamese.

When I stayed behind at recess pretending to catch up on my history assignment, Miss Fordyce asked, "Why aren't you out playing with the other children, Beverly?"

"Why aren't you in the teacher's lounge with the other teachers?"

How these girls who crowd together on this stretch of green decide who is one of them and who is not is not clear to me. Watching them so pleased to be entering this tasteful house, I ask Hannah, "Where is Bebe Lee?"

She looks surprised that I am this involved, and says, "I believe she's already inside, Mother. She's the sophomore representative, you know, and she gets to pour, so she needs to be here early."

Gathering up our skirts we step lightly over a small boxwood hedge from the wide yard onto the brick walk. Up ahead Jenny Sue and her mother, in pastel dresses, wait for us by the veranda.

"How do the girls decide they want Bebe Lee and not Cheryl?"

"Not now, Mother, *please*—" Hannah looks around to see who can hear us. Catching up with her best friend she reminds me, pleading, "You know Mrs. Garner, Mother."

3. Her Family

My mother writes a gushing letter about Hannah's engagement. She has heard all the details from Dorothy, who, as the youngest, still faithfully writes a Sunday afternoon letter home. Mother is transported back to the excitement and confidence of Dorothy's own getting pinned and then engaged to Charlie. It has been a long dry spell, clouded with my divorce, since Mother has been able to participate in a vicarious wedding. She sends Hannah a clipping from the Corpus paper showing dresses for spring brides.

She writes:

> You are our most precious link with your mother
> but a dear girl in your own right. Maybe you and
> your young man would like to come down here and
> try out our hospitality. We have two empty guest
> rooms going begging. Because of your grandfather's
> back we can't make the car trips we'd like to to see
> our girls, and they are all too busy with their own
> families to give much thought to their parents who are
> not getting any younger. When I have an excuse to
> I can still make biscuits that melt in your mouth. Let
> us hear from you and you might tell your mother
> that it has been too long a spell since she put pen to
> paper. Love,

> Grandmother Opal

Hannah is touched by the letter, which is addressed just
to her. She reads it aloud and then reads again the line:
our most precious link with your mother but a dear girl
in your own right. It brings a blush to her cheeks. "They
really love you, Mother," she says, reassured.

She decides it would be a nice thing to do to visit these
relatives who reside in Corpus Christi now; to be able to
tell Eugene and his mother that she is driving down to
visit her grandparents. To be able to show what a close,
caring family we all are. Not having a father means
Hannah does not have a whole battery of kin to gather
round her for her engagement. There should be young
aunts and cousins-once-removed and white-haired uncles
all sending their felicitations. (In the CPA's case it might
have been better if he had been born an orphan.)

She hesitates, however, about inviting her betrothed,
not sure that her grandmother's cluttered house with its
lace doilies and out-of-date furniture is somewhere that

Eugene would have a good time. He is friendly with everyone, but he is used to a little more service, and they would have to share a bath, and, not to find fault, but Grandmother talks a whole lot about when her girls were little and Eugene really doesn't know the aunts all that well.

She decides she will go alone and give them the pleasure of her company; that she can bring back lots of pictures of everyone and of the old house in Sally which has a frontier look.

After some discussion we decide that the only obstacle in her path is two slick tires on the car and we invest in two new ones to be put on the front. They are not steel-belted radials (or any other kind of radials) but Hannah resists my suggestion that Roy, if approached, could get us better tires for less.

She writes her grandmother:

Dear Grandmother Opal,

You are the sweetest thing to ask me down and I would just love to come see you and Granddaddy this weekend. You won't have to meet the bus because Mother is letting me take the car out on the highway by myself and I have promised to be very careful.

Eugene won't be able to come with me as he has an important engineering examination Monday and this is very important because he is a senior. I know you all will understand about that. Thank you very much for asking him.

I hope Granddaddy is feeling fine and I can't wait to see you all and eat those wonderful biscuits you make.

Love,
Hannah

She takes along a picture of her with her mother that was taken by a party picture service at the mother-daughter tea. We are holding hands and smiling and Hannah's face beams with pride that it is all going to be all right after all. Her mother looks uncertain. Help, her eyes say, I am trapped. But Mother will not see that: she notices only the externals. She will be overcome to see her middle daughter in a decent dress with her hair fixed as she ought to wear it all the time, and at a *sorority house* besides. Mother, Opal, has often said, ever since she first visited Mildred at the university, that if anything such as an unexpected tragedy happened to Kermit, she would really enjoy being a housemother at a sorority house. What a never-ending flow of vicarious lives—a lifetime of serenades, flowers, and rings.

Hannah is full of the responsibility of her trip. She has filled the car and got it washed at a drive-through place. Her suitcase is in the trunk and she has told me twice that she means to call Aunt Mildred and Aunt Dorothy when she gets back and tell them about seeing their mother and daddy, if it is all right with me about the phone bill. She is a missionary going down to the coastal bend to see a semi-retired druggist and the wife who looks after him. Rather, she will be a missionary on her return, bringing a helping of motherly love, thick as a bowl of mayonnaise, to spread around on the three of us.

"Be careful, honey."

"Remember Ben said to call him, Mother, if you need a car while I'm gone."

"I'll do that."

"Well, go out to lunch with your friend Clarice, too; you don't want to spend the whole time here in the house."

"I'll be fine."

She folds the map to the highway she needs and puts it on the seat beside her. "Good-by, Mother." Carefully she backs out our gravel driveway, looking both directions, and plunges determinedly into the stream of Saturday morning traffic.

With Hannah in Corpus, Ben and I have the house to ourselves. Through the high open window wind blows the scent of the warm late afternoon into my room. I am without clothes, happy to be undressed, lying close. Ben has a heavy line of hair running the length of his chest and belly; wine drips on it, which makes me want to love again.

He moves his leg against mine; we are not ready for talking. I lay my cheek against his line of hair, grateful for the privacy.

Sometimes when we touch in the bed there are many of us there: there is Charlie reaching his hand under my sweater in the car, there is the CPA with his brittle laugh, there are Ben's rounded girls who stare and stuff themselves, there is a long-ago pregnant wife.

Now there are just the two of us and we breath slowly to the same rhythm. The September sun lingers below the trees, making a glow on the ceiling. The wind dies down and it is very still: Indian summer. The high window lets in street sounds but only a glimpse of waning daylight. We lie dozing until it is twilight and cool, pleased not to have to hurry.

Ben stirs and puts a pillow under his head. "Well, it's done." He returns us to where we are.

"Was it bad to have to tell her?"

"It was bad. She never spoke." He uses a flattened tone. "At least it was my last time out there. All those zombies pulling and tugging at one another. One woman began to weep into her white gunny-sack dress and beg me to leave because I had hexed the place and now they would never get their Cream of Wheat for supper."

"What did Van say to you?"

"Nothing. Like always. She rocked back and forth like she did when the baby died and she went in and never came out. With little Van calling to her like she was in another room, pulling down her mother's face with her hands and calling to her like she was deaf. A very bad scene all the way around."

I imagine every detail of an older version of Van, Jr., imagine a woman peaked and plain, withdrawn and gray-faced. She claws at her garments, soaks them with her tears, finds words impacted in her throat. Ben, overcome, throws himself on his knees and buries his face in her institutional skirt. He implores her forgiveness. Frantically she pats at his curly hair, uttering at last a garbled sound. A voice, cracked and fragile as glass breaking on concrete, says, "Benny . . ."

I turn my face to the wall. "It must have been hard to make the break."

"She no longer exists for me, not the way she is now." He moves his leg from mine as if the contact were disloyalty, and confesses, more to himself, "I have trouble forgetting the way she used to be."

"You don't have to divorce the past."

"The past must serve some useful purpose for the present. At least there's a whole history department at the university plus two endowed chairs predicated on it. At times the connection escapes me."

"Maybe she no longer understands. Maybe she has gone so far in it doesn't reach her."

"God knows what goes on in Van's head. I never did; I only thought I did." He touches me as if being here in this bed would erase all the rest. He wraps his arms around me and holds me as close as man can get to woman, as close as two who are separate can come. We love again with my head crushed to him, my hair tangling with his.

He showers in my narrow bath, talking out his trip to Van as well as his tedious hours with the lawyer, with general comments on the foot-dragging nature of the law. He talks though the sound of water between us. It must be like hearing confession through a priest's thin wall. My mind stays on Van as he talks.

He puts a distance between him and their encounter. What he tells now is not the reality of Van locked in herself and the hospital halls but his defenses against her. The guilt she creates. He sudses himself, a man who likes to be where he is fully, immersed in the shower and the subculture. He is threatened in his beliefs by her who answers to rules she has invented for herself, going against the world's taboos.

"I got through it," he says, toweling dry, "by imagining the institution out there as something invented by Borges. Like the vague imaginary characters who inhabit his realistic halls and petty government offices, described down to the last plank on the floor. Like that one about the bar of sulphur in the drawer of a mahogany desk."

As we dress I try to tell him scraps about my family, on my mind because of Hannah's pilgrimage. Not much. The lace doilies. The back operation. Mother living our girl-hoods with us, each one in turn. Her disappointment in Beverly, who did not supply her with much that could be put in a scrapbook. All of which he must have gleaned before.

"Were your folks any worse than anyone else's? I doubt it. Mine, for example, suffered mostly from stupidity, which I understand can be hereditary."

"Does each generation have to live through the next? Do I do that with Hannah?" How many of us are in that car to Corpus?

"Relax, you're not engaged to Eugene."

He relegates the discussion to a general problem, escaping from the strain of dealing with any one particular family. He could be right. Only in story books is one lucky enough to have a cruel stepmother who sends you into the forest to the wolves, bread crumbs in your pocket to scatter for the birds. In real life things are very much alike for middle-girls of the middle class.

As I button on my dress, for we are not used to walking unclothed out of this room into the public part of the house, I offer, "We can eat in the living room."

We have lasagna and spinach salad on the coffee table. Sitting on Hannah's rug we pour more wine and listen to Verdi on the old turntable.

Over coffee he says, "Borges wrote about taking with him when he died the image of a red horse in a vacant lot, the bar of sulphur . . ."

"Yes." He will take a girl pregnant and eating sweet rolls with both hands. His image.

Marriage brings together too many people. There are Kermit and Opal and cousins-once-removed and white-haired uncles. . . It is too overwhelming to imagine a merger of all those who populate Ben's past with all of those who populate my own.

Hannah, home from her visit to Corpus, brings bubbling news of Beverly's parents. She emanates health; the faint sunburn on her face gives her the look of Heidi in the Alps. Heidi with sunbleached hair. "Oh, Mother, they talked about you all the time. You really do have to go visit, or at least write to them. They took me out to dinner at a fantastic seafood place that had the best shrimp you ever ate. Granddaddy was so sweet he said we could go anywere we wanted to and Grandmother made us chicken salad with pecans for lunch. She's really a good cook. And she wanted to know when I was going to get my ring and told me to tell Eugene he was a lucky person." She is elated to be loved and wanted by her extended family.

Opal sounds the same: pretending to be nineteen and engaged again; pumping her granddaughter for the juice of her life; spending all the time after breakfast getting ready for lunch.

"Aren't you going to ask me about them or anything? I mean, it's your own mother and daddy."

So they are. "All right, tell me how they looked. Is Daddy flat on his aching back? Has Mother become a boozing fustilugs? Are there still two struggling bougain-villea by the front door?"

Hannah's eyes cloud up. She is an open, trusting person who does not need my heavy hand.

If I have brought her this far surely I can put up with this report on the pair who began me. "Honey, I'm sorry." As if she were a small child, I kiss her cheek. "Tell me about them. Of course I want to hear, because you want to tell me."

"Well." Hannah gathers her robe around her. She is showered, getting ready to go out with Eugene whom she has not seen for three days. Her cache of hair is piled on top of her head to protect it from the water. Without it about her, like Rapunzel, she looks smaller and more easily damaged.

"Did they take you to church?" I make amends, inquiries.

"Yes, and I met their minister who is a really young man. He is nice and all that and in a way he reminded me of my civics teacher, but he wasn't the sort of person that Aunt Dorothy's minister is. I mean, he's not the sort you would want to perform the service. Grandmother said he had done the funeral for a friend of theirs and that he just missed the whole point. But I was glad they took me, anyway."

The whole point? Death? "Hmmmmmmmm." Thank God, I suppose, for Aunt Dorothy's producing a beloved elderly pastor who will marry my daughter and Eugene. It covers my own omission.

"You know, the amazing thing is how much you look like Grandmother. It isn't really something that shows up in pictures and I hadn't seen them in a long time, and it's not your features or anything but the way you look, I guess, your coloring."

The young always sink bared teeth into their elders.

62

"Other people have mentioned that." To our separate dismay.

"But what I was about to forget, gosh, I meant to show you when I came home first thing, is this picture of you and the aunts." She goes and gets her good pink linen bag, with walnut handles, that has her initials and two white flowers appliquéd on it. "I really brought it home to show Eugene. I hope you don't mind. It's really a good picture."

She hands it to me, along with two posed shots from this trip of Kermit and Opal by the bougainvillea, and Hannah standing by their newly purchased car. At nineteen, Beverly stares out between a rounded Dorothy and a vibrant Mildred. She is trim and lipsticked with a familiar prisoner's look in her eyes: help, I am trapped.

"You were really pretty, Mother. You always talk about how you weren't real cute when you were growing up, but you were." She is so proud of this paper mother in a secondhand cashmere sweater, this brief Charlie's girl.

"They didn't take pictures when I wasn't." Several hundred dowdy Beverlys were never recorded for the album.

Hannah goes on as though she didn't hear that. "Grandmother said maybe before you got married again—I hope you don't mind that I told her about you and Ben but she was just so interested in how you were doing—that you would bring him down for her to meet."

"We'll see."

Hannah hesitates in the doorway, not wanting to go too far, not wanting to tell me things that might upset me. "She s-said that she had liked my daddy very much, but that you all just weren't s-suited to one another."

"Perspicacity on her part."

"Mother—"

"Honey, it's fine."

She watches my face. "I guess I better get that letter off to Daddy and tell him about the wedding." It is a question.

Yes, I tell her, go ahead and do that. And how glad my parents were to have her down and how sweet she was to go and hurry off now and dress for her true love. Things like that. And it's a shame there isn't any wine left in the house.

Hannah's family, of course, is not my family. Opal, my mother as opposed to her grandmother, is a pushy woman who nursed her own mother through ten bedridden years and who means to make her place in the world, her world encompassing Sally and Corpus, before her time comes. My grandmother was left by her husband and to provide against a similar fate my mother got her own husband fixed up with a back so bad he couldn't leave if he had wanted to. A little insurance. Mother made some bad feelings in the family between Daddy and his brother the pharmacist over his operation; she didn't use the doctor Uncle Chester recommended, she used the one at church who sometimes passed the collection plate and who was the only doctor she had ever known who called her by her first name.

Meg, a friend from my early divorced days, observed that you weren't grown until you could forgive your parents for being your parents. She was good at one-liners. She was also the one who said on more than several occasions: men are swell but marriage is hell. Even she had problems with her mother, and later with his, too, as she got custody of her in-laws in her divorce.

It behooves me then to grow up enough, at forty, to drop them an amicable Columbus Day note thanking them for entertaining my daughter and asking Mother, perhaps in a postscript, if she would please refrain from giving her views on my past marriage, as that will not tend at all to field me into another one.

"Its family family family," Meg told me, "all your life. When I dreamed I was screwing his eighty-year-old grandfather who had his false teeth in a glass by the bed, I knew it was time to get out."

"I didn't know women could leave husbands."

"They can do anything they want to. Believe me."

"But how will you get along?"

"Watch me and take lessons."

But for a while she got on encumbered with me and very young Hannah in that old house with the rope swing. That was a nice place; the rent was dirt cheap. It made my being left seem different from my grandmother's version. It made it seem quite good fortune. I wonder what happened to the ice cream freezer we had. And to Meg.

Hannah's letter to her father would bring tears to the eyes of a decent man. He himself will crumple it into a ball and hurl it at the wall, a reminder that there is a loose end not under his control.

She writes:

> Dear Dad, In June I plan to marry Eugene Bracken who is a very fine person who plans to be an engineer. We are going to be married in a small ceremony at an Easter service by the minister of my aunt. I sincerely

hope that you can come, or if not, that if you ever get over this way to Texas you will have supper with Eugene and me.

Give my regards to your wife and little boy.

Love,
Hannah

Hannah never makes mention to me of this half-brother of hers. She never brings up the CPA either, except to tell me what she is sending her daddy for Christmas or to show me the birthday card she has bought for her daddy. What feelings she has locked up for this man who bombards her with florist's flowers once a year and never writes except to send snapshots of himself having fun with his male child who has reached the pinnacle of Little League baseball, is anybody's guess. My feelings on him are not as closely guarded.

"It's a beautiful letter."

"You're being sarcastic."

"It's my way." Write anyone you want; just don't show me.

"I just wondered if you thought it was the right thing to say to Daddy, is all." She looks hurt.

"Fine."

She hesitates, wanting things to be all right, as she has a favor to ask. "Do you think I'd have time to call the aunts? Is that still all right, I mean about the bill?"

Yes, her mother says, to all of that.

Hannah on the phone to Dorothy reminds me of her earlier excited call telling of her engagement and that we were going to buy a house, such news, and asking a very special favor of her aunt.

To me she had said, "Mother, remember what a lovely

66

Christmas we had at Aunt Dorothy's last year? Remember at that midnight service Christmas Eve how we all made a circle and passed communion and then lit candles and set them one by one on the altar? It was so beautiful. Do you think we could ask Aunt Dorothy? I mean, if maybe Eugene and I could be married in her church . . ."

Dorothy had been pleased. She would like to imagine us gathered together in her verdant house, the bride going forth from an arbor in Eden. She would want to be the one to offer us a preacher with family ties and a church small enough for our friends and gracious enough for Eugene's. Dorothy is full of kindness. She tries always to make up to us all for whatever it is we have to do without.

Hannah says on the phone, "Did I get you away from supper, Aunt Dorothy?"

And then after being reassured, she says, "I wanted to tell you what a good time I had in Corpus Christi with Grandmother and Granddaddy."

And later, then, after they have talked about the weather on the coast and how everyone's health is, Hannah inquires if it is still all right for Aunt Dorothy to fill her station wagon and drive past a lime plant and across a river to our house for the announcement party which is not very long away.

"Aunt Dorothy is so sweet and she said she'd do everything, and all the food and all the flowers and get here early and help us set it up. She is just the nicest person I ever knew."

She calls Mildred, also, because she does not want to play favorites and because for so long Mildred was the one to look after her with packages in the mail and dollars tucked in birthday envelopes. She tells her, "Grandmother and Granddaddy really do want to drive down to the valley and meet us at your house Thanksgiving, as you don't live too far from them, you know. And maybe," she says shyly into the mouthpiece, "I'll have my ring by then."

By the time she is through spreading family like a rash through the house I am out of my shoes with my feet propped up on the dining table. The dishes are not done; Ben is not coming by tonight and cannot come tomorrow night; my supervisor expects a drawing and three articles for our monthly HEXPOP newsletter by noon tomorrow; and I am weary of this wedding already and it is just the end of September.

You read that wolves mate for life; surely they decide all this in less time, a little eye-to-eye, a shoulder rub, and it is off to the cave. (Cave? Where do wolves live when they are not howling outside Zhivago's window?)

There is too much family. Perhaps I should bring up with Hannah the whole matter of wolves. We could get out the old set of World Books and read about them. "Did you know—"

"Mother?" Hannah looks nervously at me on her way to let down her locks and change her frocks. "Do you want me to help you before Eugene comes?"

"No, just be at the front door and whisk him away."

"Next week," she promises, "I'll really begin to help you get the whole house clean for my party. Do the floors and everything." She thinks over the scene. "Do you think we can afford some party napkins, the paper kind you get for parties, with our two names on them, his and mine?" She has a vision before her of what is nice as she looks past my stocking feet around our glass-walled dining room.

"Sure." My feet come down to the floor. There is still time to tidy up the kitchen and clean my hair.

"We could move the table over here and put flowers at this end."

"Fine." Even two people can constitute a family if they are both servants of the same house.

4. Her Party

Hannah has worked doggedly all week long to ready her house for her announcement party. Her white hands have coped with mops, sponges, scrub brushes, and window cleaner to prepare this room which awaits the crowd.

The living room, like a young girl making her debut, outdoes itself with charm; never has its ceiling seemed as tall or its tile frieze as brilliant. As in all fine chambers there are ghosts about. It is easy to imagine the whispers of parties long ago when the former occupant was buttoned into her party dress, on the arm of her new husband.

There would have been a fine hand-cranked Victrola by the tall window, and girls in short bobbed hair and rouged knees would have made the room crackle with the sex of arms being touched and looks exchanged.

In the days of such previous parties there would have been help in the kitchen taking tiny hot pies from an old gas oven and keeping the sauces warm in double boilers, help opening and closing the back door to get a breath of air in the cramped space. My grandmother had a cook named Ora who could do boiled custard that didn't curdle and that floated egg whites as light as clouds. Ora had large sore feet in cracked bedroom shoes, but my grandmother took no notice of that. Anyway, that was a long time ago. As long ago as when other feet danced on these waxed boards beneath our own. Dorothy assured Hannah that if you had champagne and coffee and something sweet no one would care that it was not dinner, and she has supplied it all. There are hollow-stemmed goblets on the dining table for the cooled wine, and gold-edged dessert plates that belonged to Charlie's mother. In the kitchen are three dozen sumptuous meringues filled with strawberries and lemon sauce, waiting to be garnished with whipped cream.

Hannah has made the coffee and is arranging on the table her contribution to the party: pink paper napkins with HANNAH and EUGENE printed in gold script inside a golden heart, scrapbook mementos.

Fresh potted flowers are everywhere. Yellow chrysanthemums and force-fed pink azaleas fill the fireplace and are massed by the front door and in the sparkling bay windows of the dining room. On the table they have placed cut pink and yellow blooms in an antique cut-glass bowl. Dorothy and Hannah in pastel dresses sway against the white walls, themselves like flowers.

It is hard to believe that all this grace is only for Eugene. I busy myself with spelling his name backward to see if he is in fact worthy of it. *Enegue* with its clear overtones of ingenue does not appeal to me. He is, so Hannah says, very interested in all her kin as he is an only child too and has no cousins besides. He can't wait to meet Aunt Dorothy and he wanted to hear all about the trip to Corpus.

Mother, still clinging to Hannah's visit, wants to meet him, too. She wrote:

> . . . We will do our best to stay well between now and Easter, for, if your grandfather's health permits, it is our fondest wish to see our beloved eldest grand-daughter in her long white dress. Not a line from your mother about your recent delightful stay with us . . .

"She really loves you, Mother," Hannah said, reading the letter.

Now she touches my shoulder to make contact. "Mother?" She seems anxious, like a princess in a primrose gown who has not yet been rescued by the prince, as if any number of things might still go wrong. His mother could misplace her crown and delay his leaving, his horse could go lame.

"It all looks beautiful," I tell her.

"Mother, do you want to go ahead and put your dress on? I mean, Jenny Sue and Bebe Lee are coming early, you know, because they're in the houseparty."

"Is it time?" The charade of preparation has mesmerized me. That and making anagrams of this future son-in-law's name.

"Well, you might as well because they'll probably be here in just a little bit."

All the while I have been watching the scene wrought by the tireless good intentions of my sister who, like a magician revealing a rabbit, brought this entire lavish transformation down in the back of her 1973 station wagon, Hannah has been embarrassed for me. My fallen beauty shop hair, tucked behind my ears during a day at work, my unfixed face and wrinkled shirtwaist dress with ink stains, are not part of the mother she longs to have by her side tonight.

"It won't take me long, honey. Everything really looks fine. Don't you worry."

"Aunt Dorothy is the sweetest thing, isn't she?"

The turtle neck on the aqua dress chafes my own. Buried in its folds, with my face powdered and my straggling hair turned under and spray set, I feel suitably matronly. There is some question as to whether setting out to raise someone who fits comfortably into the world is worth this ruse, this fitting myself, like a square peg in a round hole, into this beaded disguise. But I have sworn on the burden of my motherhood that for the duration of this special evening no part of the anarchy of Bananas Foster Landrum will escape to disturb my daughter.

At work today my mind wandered to this pageant; it was difficult to give my total admiration to my supervisor's editorial for our newsletter. His are always the same: doom is descending. A truth for which our office receives large grants.

"You thinking about something?"

"My daughter's getting officially engaged tonight."

"Give her my condolences."

"I'm trying to psych myself up to be ladylike."

"That's one of your tougher jobs all right," he conceded, but his mind was on his own. "Help me, will you, with this last sentence."

When they arrive at last, all the girls from high school and the sorority house, their dates, Eugene, his mother, the housemother, even Ben, they find Hannah's mother in her role, her face prepared and her manners on. Hand after hand is shaked, and over and over and over my voice says, "Thank you, honey," "How nice to see you again," "How pretty you look tonight," and "Hannah is so glad you could be here."

The girls have changed since high school. The sheets of straight hair to the waist that went with pep squad days have been replaced with hair that waves and curls to the shoulders. Their cheeks are brighter and their long dresses are slimmer and bolder, with lower fronts and backs. They look more like courtesans and less like daughters than they did at their graduation parties a year and a summer ago.

The boys as a group are as straight and quiet as Hannah's own. They look like extras hired for this party, and in a sense they are. In their shirts and ties they have been towed here to congratulate a girl they don't really know and her senior who gets each name in turn and shakes each hand with the same dutiful concentration he would give to a term paper.

I don't know where these suited, short-haired, well-mannered bland young men appear from. In Sally there were grinds, football players, and boys like Roy, who weren't going anywhere; in Hannah's high school there were freaks and jocks and goat-ropers. Now, here in our living room, there are pre-med students and business administration majors and engineers, all too much alike for me. In vain I search for one individual face.

For Hannah's old crowd of eleven inseparable girls this is a marvelous reunion. They run to each other and squeal and reminisce about times that are gone: that last slumber party, the big game against Reagan, the bus trip to Corpus, the time they all cut school and went to the hospital when Jenny Sue's mother had a hysterectomy. But after the first minutes of hugging and being together again they grow slightly ill at ease with one another. Their roads have forked; those who are at junior colleges and getting ready to go to work next year do not speak in the same syntax as Hannah and Jenny Sue's new friends from last year's pledge class.

The greatest change is that Cheryl and Bebe Lee, both invited by Hannah who wants very much for them to get to be friends now, are no longer the center of the stage. Each still confidently shakes her curls, demurely shows her generous breasts, and smiles a lot and blinks eyes as large and dewy as a Maybelline ad, but not even the well-tailored boys give them undue attention. Time has changed taste, and now the crowd clusters around the two girls who went off to school in Virginia who have a surface polish that makes the local girls seem overdressed and full of bygone chatter.

Loyally Hannah poses for a picture between Bebe Lee and Cheryl. She poses for one with her best friend Jenny Sue who is to be maid-of-honor. And one with Eugene and his mother. And one with Dorothy who beams like the fairy godmother she is. And another one with her own mother in the sorority-tea, engagement-party dress. These are scrapbook pictures to show whom Hannah loves and is really close to, for thumbing back through and getting a lump in her throat about, when she looks back on how special it all was and how thrilled and excited she was on the threshold of her life.

She ought to have her father here. The CPA was always one for proving what a great time was had by all. He could flash a cheerful souvenir picture of days that had at the time been vales of tears from start to finish. I think of that when we get the annual Christmas snapshot of him and his grinning Little Leaguer.

Eugene opens the first champagne bottle, carefully aiming the cork away from the window, and he and Hannah drink a toast. They both sip timidly, neither at home with alcohol. The bubbling wine brings circles of color to Hannah's cheeks and she looks her loveliest for the toasting picture, which is taken with Jenny Sue's Instamatic.

Eugene, on his way to becoming my son, is not an unpleasant boy. You can tell, looking at him, that he has done what was expected of him all his life, that he has worn gloves and a coat in cold weather, and turned his papers in on time, and always brushed his teeth after meals. You would suspect that he has a doting mother by the way he conveys politeness and fealty to his elders. He is a brown-haired, brown-eyed, leather-shoed boy with an air of not backing down from what has to be done.

It is hard to guess, looking at him, what sort of balding man he may evolve to: the apathetic kind who worries over his intestines or the red-faced kind who chases all the skirts because he feels cheated by his clean youth.

But the real unknown is what happens when two strangers like Eugene and Hannah marry. There is such a blank space in my experience between this diffident rapture, this wanting to belong to one another, and that day years ahead when Hannah looks at these snapshots and weeps for what she thought life would be. It is impossible for me to imagine the process by which a farmer's boy named Kermit, a friendly boy from the sandy sorghum fields, and Opal, the sweetheart of her consolidated county high school, became the parents of the three of us.

If, by chance, marriage is the transmuter of the one to the other, then this evening is less than an occasion for joy.

Jenny Sue comes up and squeezes my aqua waist. She is a small, dark girl with a twelve-year-old's face, who thinks we are much closer than we are "Oh, Mrs. Landrum, everything is just beautiful. It really is."

"My sister did all this—"

"She sure is nice. Hannah is always talking about her and it has been great to finally meet her. You know I hadn't met her before, in all this time." But she wants me to have credit, too. "I know you did most of the work, anyway. And it's your house and that's something to really be proud of."

"Thank you, Jenny." I search for what she wants to hear, which is not hard; it is like patting a dog, a reflex takes over. "It means so much to Hannah to have you in her house party and in her wedding. You girls have been friends as long as I can remember."

She smiles a child's smile. "It's the most exciting thing in the world to get to be her maid-of-honor. It's a dream of mine that it's hard to believe is coming true."

Out of words, we smile our smiles and watch Hannah.

"Do you think," Jenny Sue tries again, "that we could all wear pink in the wedding? Different shades of it?"

"That sounds fine. Why don't we ask Dorothy? She will have ideas for the whole wedding, I know."

Dorothy is pleased to talk about the smallest details of the bridesmaids' dresses and their bouquets and what flowers to have at the reception at the country club. Jenny Sue moves off, content.

In August Dorothy promised Hannah on the phone, "I'll do everything. And you've got that fabulous living room, I hear. Just pick a date while the weather's still pretty and things are blooming and I'll do everything. I never do anything for you all. Honestly."

"Oh, Aunt Dorothy, that would be really sweet."

"And we can write it up for the paper. I know mothers like his and they expect a big write-up in the paper."

"Oh, Aunt Dorothy, would you?"

Dorothy provides always what I cannot for my daughter: *nice*. It is a shame that all I've ever given Dorothy in return was Charlie.

We sisters sit down to visit in a corner where we can hear over the high-pitched laughter.

"This reminds me," Dorothy says, edging out of her tight shoes with relief, "of those parties Charlie and I used to give when we lived in that upstairs apartment on Rio Grande street, while he was still in school. Didn't you and Roger come once? I don't mean this house reminds me—it is really fabulous—but everybody being so young."

"You were just Hannah's age."

Somewhat wistfully she remembers. "We didn't have anywhere near enough furniture then and everybody had to sit on the floor and all we could afford was beer. And nobody was on a diet then and I baked a double batch of brownies every Saturday morning."

"The reason this reminds you is because Roger spent the whole night we came taking pictures."

She giggles. "You're right. I'd forgotten what a camera nut he was. Didn't he even take one of you all getting divorced?"

"Ben doesn't own a camera."

We laugh, and I realize how satisfactory it is to mention Ben as someone I can lay claim to. It keeps there from being anything between Dorothy and me. In my head I try one step further: my husband Ben doesn't own a camera.

"It's just wonderful to meet him."

"He's having a fine time." We look over at Ben in the midst of a nosegay of flowering girls. He is enjoying this engagement ceremony to the fullest and has immersed himself with zeal into their language and scent and moist-lipped aura.

"Don't you think he acts almost like Hannah was his own daughter?"

"He has one of his own—"

"Is she here?" Curiously she looks over the flock of girls about him.

"No, she's off at school." Impossible to imagine Van, Jr., here. She would take one look in the door and flee in terror.

"He asked me all about my roses and my garden. He just couldn't have been friendlier. Just wait until the napkins say BEN and BEV."

The fantasy of my husband Ben evaporates at such a

thought. "We may elope instead, run off to Mexico in the dead of night."

She is tickled. "I'll bring you over a ladder." She settles back into her chair, relaxed, as there is no one here, no mother, no eldest sister, no husband, to mind that showing from her butter-yellow tent dress are white arms marbled with fat. Her bosom and throat look as young as Hannah's and her soft face is as pretty as it was at nineteen, but her near and dear click their tongues because she is too lenient with herself, although accepting that she is more lenient still with all of them.

Ben comes over to us and comments audibly, "She's too good for that lump of boy."

"Shhh . . ." Dorothy giggles.

"He has said nothing but 'Yes, sir,' and 'No, ma'am,' all night."

"He isn't deaf," I suggest.

"Don't be too sure he has any of his faculties." He kneads my hand and flirts a minute with my younger sister.

A great desire comes over me to be a woman with him. This is all very well—this evening for which we bought the yellow stucco house, this evening with all the food and flowers and Hannah's glowing gratitude for our providing this propriety, this decency—but now I am ready to be out of this dress, far away from napkins embossed with gold hearts.

But there are signs that it will soon be time to wash up the plates, and Ben is heading for the door. The rite has been observed.

"He sounds just like a father already," Dorothy says when he is gone. She is pleased her sister has a man; she does not have to feel guilty about hers.

"You'll be going through this with Dottie one of these days."

"You can bet that Charlie is already practicing for it. He all but carries a shotgun to the door now."

"Will you have to do this four times? Or only for the girls?"

"Maybe some of them will elope, like you said." She doesn't believe that for a minute, but her one little boy and her three school-age girls are a long way off from leaving home. They are still eating her brownies and doing whatever the young do that is called acting-up by their parents.

It is a joke on me that, making my living advocating zero population growth, I have been given a combined total of eight nieces and nephews.

Eugene's mother descends as Dorothy slips off to say a last word to Hannah. She has seized this pause to make personal contact with the mother of her son's choice. "Beverly, isn't it?" She is coached and prepared. Mrs. Bracken is one of those undistinguished women who have learned to present a formidable and expensive front. If divested of her mauve dress with its satin-lined sweater and matching shoes, she would look exactly like my former butcher's wife, a bulky, loud woman who swept up his sawdust floor.

She says, "You must come have coffee with me soon and let us get better acquainted." She adjusts her fine sweater about her hefty shoulders. "Hannah tells me that the pastor at your sister's church will do the ceremony. Do let us know the number of family and friends we may include."

"Yes, Hannah loves that little church. We have gone

there for years for candlelight communion on Christmas Eve."

"She told me."

I make several promises expected of me concerning the ceremony and my part in it and my willingness to live up to my share. In return she exhibits the utmost tact concerning the problem of the invitations. It is apparent to us both that these may have to be done by hand—such a personal touch—as the name of the bride's mother may be subject to last-minute change. As she has been advised on this matter and has resolved to be polite, we end up talking, in full view of the assembled, as allies who have every reason to be satisfied with this union.

"I wish Eugene's father were alive to be here tonight."

"You've done a fine job of raising your son."

"He's a dependable boy." She squares those shoulders. "I can say he's never given me a moment's trouble."

"You must be proud."

"Hannah is certainly a dear girl."

"She's very loyal."

"I'm sure."

We act as a receiving line to tell everyone good night. It has been an exciting evening for all the girls who haven't been together in so long. Now they are turning their pretty faces to their dates and thinking about the part of the evening parked in the car. There is more hugging all around and lots of promises to really get together again real soon.

"She certainly has lots of friends," Eugene's mother admits.

Exhaustion limits me to a smile.

Hannah is suffused with relief and joy when we have a minute alone as Eugene sees his mother to her car.

"Wasn't it all right?" I ask her.

"Oh, Mother, it was just perfect. It was the happiest evening of my life."

"Everyone liked Dorothy's fancy dessert."

"It was just wonderful. And you were, too, Mother. And Eugene's mother really liked you, I could tell. Don't you think she's really an interesting person?"

"We got on fine."

"It was awful that Aunt Dorothy had to drive back home by herself in the dark."

"She didn't mind. She wants to do this. I told her you'd bring the dishes up this weekend because she needed to get home."

"She's just the sweetest person in the world. And I thought she looked beautiful, even if she is sort of overweight, didn't you?"

Eugene comes back in to say good night. "It sure was a good party, Mrs. Landrum. Thanks a lot for giving it. My mother said to remind you that you promised to come over and have coffee with her some time."

"Thank you, Eugene." I lean up and give him an awkward kiss, to cement the evening. We are both nervous from it, but Hannah flushes with approval.

She says, "Ben had a good time, too, didn't he?"

"He enjoyed it."

"He really is a nice person, Mother." She and Eugene look at each other, wanting us all to be as betrothed as they are.

"He is. Everything was." Everything was *nice*. And I cannot bear another minute of it.

"We won't be gone long, Mother. Eugene wants to be sure that his mother gets home okay, so, if it's okay, we're going to follow her home and then I'll be back."

"Take your time, honey."

"Just leave the dishes, now. We won't be long." She makes the gesture although she does not doubt that the stacks of heirloom plates gummy with lemon sauce and cream will all be washed up and put away when she returns.

"Good night, Mrs. Landrum, and thank you again."

"Yes, Eugene. Good night."

I put my feet up on my shelf-table and savor the absence of all those others. Ignoring for a time the messy plates and forks and cups and coffee grounds, I savor a final cup of dark, strong coffee.

As if on signal, Roy lets himself in the door. "They left you with it, huh?"

"Looks that way."

"Where's the prof?"

"He stuck it out until eleven."

"And where did the princess go? I saw him open the door for her and help her in the car and fasten her seat belt. What a rube."

"They are following Eugene's mother home."

"Jesus."

"Hannah won't be happy to see you here."

"Tell me something I don't know." He leans back in his chair against the wall. "She had the whole gang it looked like."

"Some of them I hadn't seen since high school."

"I recognized a couple. The ones who balled around a

little, the cheerleaders. Recognized those screaming voices. Sounded like my sister's crowd but you could tell the difference when they all came out and got in their boy friends' daddies' Oldsmobiles."

"How long have you been out there?"

"About an hour." He is pleased with himself for spying on Hannah's big evening. For having sat right across the street with his lights off, his radio on country rock, and his window down so he could hear the noise.

"Want dessert? There are a few left."

"Why not?" He finds the uneaten meringues and heaps two on an already used gold-rimmed plate. He pours himself some coffee.

We open our window to a night as still and black as a cat. There are no stars or moon out for Hannah's engagement, only this warm dark sky. It shouldn't be so—there is no reason for it—but Roy's appearance has the air of the clandestine. I find myself listening for Eugene's car on the gravel drive or Ben's key in the front lock. There should be no difference from having coffee at midnight or having iced tea at noon.

He cleans his plate and puts it back on the stack. While he is up he wanders into the rest of the house, checking out the scene we've laid to impress the visitors. He remarks on its general resemblance to a funeral home with all the flowers stuck around. "You put on the dog for sure," he says, back in his chair again.

"For Eugene's mother."

"Her type would be built like a cement mixer and dripping diamonds. Right?"

"Only one ring. But her shoes were dyed to match her dress."

He looks me over. "You got your hair squirreled up again, didn't you? She make you do that?"

"It's my gesture."

"Why're you still in that fancy dress?"

"Well, they just left—"

"And I won't shove off, you're saying. Don't worry, I'll be gone when they get back."

"I've got to clean up."

"You're scared she'll blow her top."

"Something like that."

He takes one last look around, and, with a few comments on my daughter's putting on airs, fades down the street in a squeal of rubber.

Hannah says when she comes in ten minutes later, "Oh —I'm glad you decided to leave everything, Mother. Let me just change out of my dress and all and I'll come help you."

"Go on to bed, honey. I was just getting into my robe. It won't take me long to rinse these off."

"Well, if you're sure . . ." She gives me a grateful hug. "Thank you for everything, Mother."

"You had a nice party." To which I wish I had not been invited.

Two: Foster

5. Her Work

The office where I work is a small information and referral agency within walking distance of town, the capitol, and the university. As well as lending or selling such books as *The Population Bomb, Famine 1975, Education and Catastrophe, Affluence in Jeopardy, A Blueprint for Survival, Resources and Man,* and *Limits to Growth,* my supervisor and I get out a monthly newsletter with items on the population problem clipped from the current pages of numerous bulletins, reports, and magazines to which we subscribe. In addition, two or three times a year I design and reproduce a special flyer, to send to all those on our mailing list, which tries to make an overwhelming statistic understandable by showing it in a different context, one more familiar, more ordinary.

When you deal with the reality of a world which is crowding itself to the edge of survival, with problems such as the inevitable water shortage and disposal of human wastes implicit in a population heading in the next thirty years toward seven billion, you deal with numbers of such size and pessimism that the public shuts them out. My job at my desk, clipping and pasting, is to try to prevent this dodging of reality; our larger job at HEXPOP (Halt Exponential Population Growth) is to effect through changes of attitude some small stemming of the tide of overpopulation.

It is an uphill task; none of us as we are is ready to face up to the problem. Even while I work on putting together our newsletter I take for granted that our own house has two bathrooms for two persons, that even as the world's fossil fuels dwindle we still drive our car with its air conditioner running.

HEXPOP's sober but concrete program, slow-moving as it is, is very different for me from the early picketing, marching, and boycotting that I did during the years of my marriage to the CPA. At that time in our lives we women found it exhilarating just to make noise and carry banners, to be involved in an overt act of protest. We picketed, for example, Sabrosa Melons, which had acquired the reputation of being the largest, most influential, most unfair plantation in the valley. Wearing our flat shoes and sunglasses, and scarves against the heat, we stood guard in shifts of two in front of the grocery stores, to protest the working conditions under which the fruit was grown and harvested. We rose to outrage at the sight of women who continued to select from golden pyramids the ripe cantaloupe marked with Sabrosa stickers.

Although, with help from California, gains were made in this area later by the unions, our efforts, as those of most of our causes then, resulted in the failure we had come to expect, almost to seek, as it seemed proof that we were on the side of truth, that we were the righteous opposition. Now we and the world are older and it is in too serious a shape for us to tilt at windmills. Now we are compelled to work daily to the end that we bring about a decent measure of real change.

The satisfaction in this job is that, as Miss Fordyce instructed me, it deals with what is important. Our belief is that every child should have food to eat and space to grow; our goal is to brake the exponential births of children, to stop such catastrophes as the inexorable sweep of starvation across the arid planes of Africa and India.

Fifteen years ago our office did not have the money it requested nor the national recognition it sought. Fifteen years ago organizations such as ours still spoke in terms of "every child a wanted child," not realizing that too many decent people were overcrowding with too many wanted children. As the problem has accelerated our attempted solutions have altered, so that now when we have funds for all we try to do, we are unable to do any of it fast enough.

When I was living with Meg and looked for a job with no credentials but a college degree and a hungry preschool child, I counted heavily on being in the eleemosynary heart of Texas, saw myself mothering the battered child, the alcoholic, the homeless, the disabled: it seemed a natural step for someone with a bleeding heart and a back-ground in lost causes.

Meg protested that if all I was going to do was serve coffee and be a shoulder to cry on I might as well marry again. "Program computers," she insisted. "Machines can be unplugged when you want to take a bath."

This office came my way because Henry, my supervisor, whose goal then as now was to impress the feds, wanted someone who would put together a few brochures; and I, in a fit of desperation on my application blank, remembering *The Making of Bananas Foster*, had listed writing as my interest. I can also read, which pleases him even more, as this provides him with all the up-to-date facts which cross our desks. So this arrangement has been of mutual benefit.

My desk is in what could be called a reception area, as you first come in our door from a second-floor hall. Henry is around the corner, and therefore out of sight of the transient and curious who walk in, which necessitates my going to get him when he has a caller, much as if I were his secretary. He does not protest this arrangement.

In addition to the desk, I have a hard chair with rollers, a file cabinet which is half my own, and a window. It is essential to have a window to look out, for reality testing, to know whether it is wet or dry, gray or clear, scorching or blowing. It doesn't look distinctive, this space of mine, but it gives me pride to be here. Certain scraps of Foster are visible: between two metal bookends are two dictionaries; my glasses case is in a Mason jar with some pencils; three pots of ivy sit on the window sill; there is a cork bulletin board that displays my folders.

Today I am dealing with the fact that in the next decade we will find parts of Latin America with 150,000 starving children. The challenge is to put the consequences of too many of us on too small a planet into terms possible to assimilate, to put the implications into a daily context so that there is impact in the contrast, but impact which can be absorbed. The problem is to make it reach the reader in such a way that it is not shut out, the way you turn quickly through the magazines which show starving young faces staring at you across the page from ads for Steuben glass.

I have experimented with one pasted and sketched hypothesis of how it could be when there are more children than can be claimed or cared for; it is an attempt to juxtapose the unexpected so that my fact about the Latin-American children hits home.

On the inside of the folder is an actual photograph of the local dog pound with the dogs standing on hind legs in their metal pens—a Labrador, a poodle, three bony hounds —and below that a notice explaining for how long dogs will be kept unclaimed before being put up for sale, or, if unwanted, put to the gas. On the facing page is a collage of children's faces, cut from magazines, about fifteen in all, staring over one another's shoulders behind a drawn-in pen, with the same notice below only this time the word *child* is substituted for *dog*. On the front cover is the fact, enclosed in a box, with no comment; on the back cover is our office address and a blank for obtaining information, or, of course, sending money. For a while I debate adding somewhere the actual small number of calls the woman at the Humane Society told me they got on missing dogs and the vast number no one ever comes to claim . . . but there does not seem to be a need to belabor my point.

This is not the first time I have tried an idea like this.

95

Last year about this time, at the start of deer-hunting season, I did one using a photograph which drew on a local situation. It is the custom here to strap dead bucks onto the hoods of cars after a hunt; by the end of November there are cars all around the state with deer roped to their radiators. Across from a picture of one I pasted up a dead child bound to the grill of an identical car. Trying to show the enormity of this when it is put into human terms, beneath the deer picture I used an actual quote from the sports section of our paper giving the rationale that if the deer population is not "mercifully thinned out" by hunters the deer will die of starvation. Then, similarly to the dog-pound folder, I substituted *child* for *deer* beneath the mock-up. It got a lot of feedback, not the quietest being the threat of a lawsuit from the sports writer whose words I had cribbed.

Both of these are attempts to show that so much we do today to those we consider lesser—animals here, countless lives in Southeast Asia—lies in wait for us in our future as we press closer and closer against one another.

Most of my earlier folders which showed actual conditions, such as rats in the temples of India drinking fresh milk from sacred vessels while babies starved on the streets, were too harsh and were received in silence, as readers in self-defense made themselves as immune to them as they had to the knowledge of napalm in the war.

Today's folder will be done on paper the harsh yellow of traffic warnings; the deer one last year was done on fresh-cut red.

Henry says, "I'll look it over. You want to rustle up some coffee?"

Henry and I work well together in that we both give our

job top priority. This was not the case when I first started here as I had neither worked before nor been around a man all day before. His approval was essential to me, and when we sat together over coffee I imagined electricity in the air between us. But as we got to be old hat to each other, like people underfoot in your own house, my emotional investment dwindled and this office became important to me apart from him. It became the one consistent place where I was Foster rather than Hannah's mother, just as, for Henry, this is the one place where he does not have to account to his wife. Which makes us tackle our work with the same affection.

Henry has an unparalleled ability to sell our program. He conveys, despite his calamitous predictions, such an air of confidence, implying that if he is only followed like a stocky Pied Piper from an agriculture and mechanical college, we will all be rescued in the end. His editorials have been reprinted in such house organs as ZPG's *National Reporter,* his letters to the editors have appeared in newspapers around the state, and he has been on TV from time to time locally to explain the world's predicament. In those situations, to demonstrate his credentials, he presents himself as an agronomist, as an authority on the world's tillable and arable lands. Which actual soil, he, like my father, has arranged to stay as far away from as possible.

When he speaks out on those signposts and landmarks of the population fight, his style is to point out that whatever is being done is too little and too late. Last year for example, taking my condensations of the facts, he did a piece chastising the delegates from 114 countries to the UN Conference on Human Environment for spending their time on nationalistic trivialities; and another that lambasted the President of the United States for making no recommendation or even comment on the Report of the President's Commission on Population Growth and the American Future.

As Henry is attending our national conference Saturday, a new brochure is essential, a shocking visual to impress the feds. On the lookout for fresh grants he will put our year's best pieces before every eye.

"What made an Aggie like you get into this job, Henry?" I asked him when I started work.

"Shirley was nagging me to get a government job so we could live where her folks live. But I didn't get a college education to be one of your little cogs in the wheel. Besides, you only have to raise a few cows and turn a few fields," he insisted, having done neither, "to see there isn't enough of your land to go around."

We both tone down our real concern. You can't let it get out of hand and still come to work day after day.

"This is terrific," he pronounces about my folder. "It'll be the best thing at that whole dog and pony show in New York. No danger of the Humane Society suing, is there?" He remembers the sports writer.

"I haven't said anything libelous about them."

"Terrific. What gave you this idea?"

"When I was at the beauty shop, back before Hannah's party, there was this woman who kept telling how she'd lost her Lhasa apso and how she'd been down to the pound three times to look for him."

"And you put it on the back burner to stew?"

"Something like that."

"Print up a thou and I'll take half of them with me."

"After lunch. I'm meeting Ben."

"No hurry. I'll put the polishing touches on my talk. Say, what made you pick this yellow paper?"

A norther has struck during the morning and at noon Ben and I, unprepared, bend against the cold wind. We go down the mall, past polling booths, sidewalk revivalists, Hare Krishna singers, placards by the student publications against the Board of Regents: all the usual and familiar trappings of education. Ben delights in it all; he takes all the handouts we are offered. Crossing the Union patio we squeeze through two dozen blue-jeaned students who are listening to a guitarist. No one moves to make way for us. I look at the faces, each so different, most very young, a few bearded, drawn close together in the cold by a sound like Ravi Shankar.

"You should have brought a sweater." Ben tucks my arm through his.

"It was eighty-five degrees this morning."

"You ought to keep one at your office. I had one, but someone lifted it."

Seated at our table he complains, "Why do we eat at this place? This isn't meat loaf, it's pressed cereal."

"You want to trade?" I offer my knockwurst and cabbage.

"That's worse."

We are crowded against a post in a corner table. "Everyone is here today. It must be too cold to walk up the street."

He inspects his colleagues. "Mostly educators and engineers. They have no taste buds. They'll eat whatever leftovers anybody serves." With reluctant hunger he tackles his plate lunch. Although he never likes the food—last week it was salmon loaf—he always eats it with gusto. He is like a student in a boardinghouse, complaining as he cleans his plate, because that's a part of what is expected in the setting.

It doesn't bother me as long as I don't project myself into the cook's place. If that were my meat loaf being eaten . . .

"It can't take longer than a couple more months," he says, pushing his clean blue plate away.

"Is that what the lawyer says?"

"Can't ever get him on the phone. But I know lawyers: they have a feel for such nuances as when the money is running out. He won't let litigation drag on when it isn't profitable."

"Maybe he considers you legal aid."

"Maybe I consider him . . . never mind." He stacks my plate on his. "Why don't you get us some more coffee?"

I do, which means going through the line again. When we have our fresh cups, he says, "I called Van, Jr., since she won't answer my letters."

"How did that go?"

"About like I expected, very negative. Nothing gets to that girl. I could have told her I was moving in with a boy. Anyway, she said she'd come down for spring break."

"What did she say about maybe getting a new mother?"

"Nothing. She remembers you. She doesn't care."

"I like Van. She knows what is real."

"That's good that you do, since I told her she could stay with you when she comes." He stirs sugar into his coffee. "I don't see her the way you do; to me she's farther off base than any kid in any one of my classes."

He applies himself to his bread pudding, putting the raisins in a separate pile and then giving in and eating the raisins. He digs for a cigarette and settles down. "We might as well stay here and talk; my office is a public hallway."

It seems a good time to show the dog-pound flyer. Spread out on the table, still in its pasted form, it looks arresting, which was the idea.

"Do you think that's in the best of taste?" He squints at the collage of children.

"Is it supposed to be tasteful, something this grim?"

"You know more about that. Doubtless they'll like it in New York."

"Henry is taking it with him, and the deer-hunting one."

"That fellow uses you, as I have said numerous times. If there is all that loose money lying around for trips you should be the one to go. He just wants to peddle his ass for a bigger share of the pie up there."

"He doesn't think we'll be hurt by the new cuts in federal funds."

He scowls at this reminder. "Here we spend billions of dollars on the military and pennies on what counts." In his role as archetype average liberal he is offended when the government is not behaving in what he considers our best interest. His ordinary face, ringed with thinning curly hair mirrors his distress; he looks like a citizen speaking out on TV.

Preoccupied, he looks again at the folder. "What happened to the ones you used to do?"

"People can't deal with truth straight on. If you ever once have empathy for a single woman, standing by a dried-up field, with dried-up breasts, you can't bear it."

"You personalize too much."

"How absurd, Ben, to say you mustn't personalize persons."

"You have to be able to look at the overview. It's the professional device that enables you to get things done." He asks defensively, "Should I have spent all my time bleeding for the catatonic inmates in Van's hospital?"

"I don't know. Should you? Should we?"

He dodges that. "Take encouragement that the birth rate was down last year."

"That isn't enough. You know that."

But he is not comfortable with the idea that all of us could be in jeopardy; it is a larger, universal truth which goes against his view that this is a world where anything is permissible within the context of its own culture.

He hands me back the brochure and finishes my half-eaten bread pudding. When he is through he places the two dessert bowls in a neat row, like students in a classroom, and grabs my hand, "Forget all that. What are our chances for tonight?"

"Hannah is going to supper with Eugene's mother and his favorite aunt."

"We'll have time; I'll come early." He squeezes my hand. "We'll do it every night," he promises himself, not lowering his voice, "when I move in. This divorce can't take forever."

"Even if it does, Hannah will be gone by summer."

"Let's go." He gathers his stuff. "This cabbage smell is like an institution and I've had enough of that." He says what he ritually says, "Remind me not to eat here again."

Downstairs in the corridor by the glass door students and faculty crowd together in no hurry to hit the chilling air;

those who have them zip into windbreakers or pull on sweaters. Behind the red-roofed buildings the sky is a dark slate gray.

"Thank you for lunch, Ben."

"You don't have to say that every time. If I'm planning to sponge off your house payments, you might as well cadge all the free meals you can. If we ever get those girls of ours out of college we'll be rich."

"Don't press your luck. I'm considering marriage at least."

"I'll press more than that." He kneads my fingers. "Keep the rollaway warm."

Henry has a visitor from the welfare office, one of those women with civil service rank who can't be bothered with the rest of us women without it. She has been here several times before. "Is he in?" she asks with a wave of her hand, relegating me to receptionist or file clerk. "Should have left my number the other day for him to call but I never know where I'll be or how long. Always in and out." She looks somewhere over my head as she talks, as if she were watching her professionalism in a mirror.

I take her around the corner to Henry's chamber, where he is checking the newsletter and adding his editorial comments. He says to her, "Glad to see you, come on in," and to me, "You want to get us some coffee?"

The visitor finally leaves, a loquacious woman in a purple bonded slack suit with a matching scarf. Henry reports that she was interested in learning about our entire operation as she is considering using us for referrals. "Looked like she was going to stay all day, didn't it? Could you hear that voice?"

He outlines what he wants to have with him at the conference that we should be locating right away: the newsletters for the last year, the two flyers, copies of his letters to the editors, anything, anything at all that can be found.

The most pressing thing we discover is a federal form which was supposed to have been sent in a month ago. He came across it, he says, in a folder with his non-profit mailing permit, which has been misplaced. It is a four-page, single-spaced, impossible-to-decipher questionnaire intended to inform an impatient bureaucracy of those matters they should already have on record in five places. It is, as he says, thirty days past due. "If you wouldn't mind tending to this. This is your typical bureaucratic b.s."

It takes over two hours with the checkbook and scraps of notes and him dictating and me translating and typing. Then there is still the new folder to get to the printers and loose ends to tie.

"Let's take a break," he says, "we deserve it."

"Coffee?"

"Can't put any more on my stomach just now."

"I'll bring you a big orange drink from the Coke machine."

He smiles broadly on receiving it, a reminder of his boyhood. With the phone off the hook we go over it all again; Henry is now checking everything twice to be sure nothing else is left undone. He discusses the bills that have to be paid this fiscal year, and the newsletter schedule for the rest of this calendar year. He talks of his trip and how much rides on the impression he makes. "Don't worry about that, Foster, I'll carry my own weight."

"Ben didn't like his meat loaf at lunch."

"Why do you eat at those second-rate dining rooms?"

"What if he doesn't like my cooking?"

"If I can stay alive on Shirley's, he'll survive. Raw potatoes are her specialty."

"You married her anyway."

"Who can remember all that?" He rubs his jaw. "Her mother was one helluva cook, I'll say that."

"False advertising."

"In more ways than one." He lets that go. "I'm leaving early today; if I don't take her out for a steak with all the trimmings then it'll be a cold Christmas at my house. She doesn't think much of these trips to the big city with her left back here. You won't mind getting the form in the mail and the new stuff to the printers, will you? It's right on your way home."

"I like it here; it's quiet. You go ahead."

He leaves with a full briefcase to impress Shirley with the workload necessary for this trip. "You want things quiet you better lock the door." To show that he is on top of things, he adds, "You don't think that yellow paper's too loud?"

I wonder if, married, I will hurry home from the office, Ben's wife, to Ben and the house, much as now I do as Hannah's mother to Hannah and the house, wondering what's to fix for supper and if things are picked up.

Hannah has had no note, letter, phone call, or comment from her daddy in response to her warmhearted letter. Tonight, her hair full as carded lamb's wool, in a new pale gold dress she has made for the occasion, she brings this up before she goes out to eat with Eugene's mother's maiden sister, who is Eugene's favorite aunt. This supper is even more of a family affair than the Sunday dinners to which she is now routinely invited.

"You had a call from Clarice, Mother," she says when I get in from work. Waiting for Eugene, she has straightened the living room and decorated it with the last two chrysanthemums from her party.

"Oh yes. Clarice. I'll get in touch with her tomorrow." Tired, I find my kitchen chair and some tea. Not in the mood for this matter which needs to get cleared up one of these days.

"She said she would call you at work."

"Yes, fine."

"Eugene is coming at seven." She looks at my dress.

"Ben took me to lunch." I am not moving.

"He's nice to do that, isn't he? He told me, you know, to come by his office anytime I was around that part of the campus."

"Good, do that."

"I plan to because he seemed to sincerely mean it. But it's hard just to walk right up to a professor's door. He might be having a conference or something."

"He'd like to see you." Like to have a sorority girl look over his posters of the Maoris and Zuni. The contrast would delight him. Ben's work lends itself to these interruptions, as all trivia for him is part of the scent of civilization. Thinking of work, I tell her, "I did a new flyer today."

"That's good, Mother. I bet Mr. Moore was pleased." She has no interest in seeing it; if it pleases my supervisor, that is sufficient. My involvement in the world is not in her frame of reference; her problems are closer to her.

"He was." I let it go.

"Mother?" Seeing that I am still sitting, she comes where I am and waits.

"What?" Reluctantly I lay down the afternoon paper.

"Do you think Dad got my letter?"

"Possibly."

"I mean, he might have a new address since he last wrote. They might have a new house by this time. Maybe he lost my envelope and wrote to our old address or something?"

Maybe I could wring his big red rooster's neck. "Would you like to call him?"

"That would be such a big phone bill, wouldn't it? And anyway, you know, somebody else might answer the phone." She looks toward the front door, hearing the bell. "Anyway, I just wondered what you thought, Mother."

I think he'll maybe add a one-line postscript on his Christmas card. "Is it okay if I don't come in there?"

"Sure, Eugene will understand." She is relieved. "We won't be out late."

"Take your time." Ben is counting on this favorite aunt a lot.

As I shower for him, and change into my jeans, which are not the skinny black jersey dress that Ben would relish, but which will come off just as quickly, I think about this Clarice.

Not the real Clarice, of course, who will turn out to be an inevitable clerical error in my life, but a Clarice who might be reaching out in friendship to Foster, another one of us who drives a standard transmission car and wears a shirtwaist dress and is known as the one female in the family who has to work.

She could be the woman in the black shoes. The woman

in black shoes is a stranger to me, and, like all strangers, we overlap each other and have for over a dozen years. When Hannah started school she was there, outside the first-grade room every afternoon to wait for her little boy, wearing black flats, black skirt, a black bulky plastic shoulder bag. When her son came out, needing to go to the bathroom, she held his hand all the way to the car. Now, much later, I see her often, in the same shoes, same bag, black slacks, with her shoe-polish hair which was then chopped above her ears, and now hangs in ropes, just behind or just ahead of me on voting day at the same precinct, or in the same grocery checkout line.

You can imagine her finally deciding to break out of that closed existence that went from first-grade days, her son in hand, to the present. (And what of him? Where do such six-year-olds go? Is he at Harvard? In jail?) It is possible that she might now be making calls from her loneliness to a similar, harried, familiar walk-on: me. "Foster, Foster, this is Clarice. Help me out. Go with me to buy navy shoes, not too great a step at once, but a step, some navy shoes. Foster . . ."

There are so many of us, Fosters and Clarices: there is a whole world of us each calling out. A woman in China calls to me. A woman in Ecuador.

6. Men

Ben stops by for breakfast and catches us by surprise. I am dressed but in my stocking feet, grabbing coffee on my way to work; Hannah has drifted in with the bloom of morning on her face, wrapped in a cornflower blue robe given her by Mildred for her birthday.

"Am I too late to eat?" he asks, sitting down with us at the table in the dining room.

It comes to me that before too long he may be here like this every morning at breakfast, although coming unshaven out of our room to sit down at this very table with the morning paper, wanting to know what there is to eat.

As he accepts a cup of coffee, I make some quick pancakes, and fry some bacon, very pleased to have some in the house. As there is no honey or syrup, I sprinkle the pancakes with powdered sugar and roll them like crepes around a spoonful of soft margarine. He is very pleased.

Pouring a second cup and fetching my shoes, I wish I had brushed my hair and had not put on these wool slacks which are only for work and the passerby.

Hannah is shy in his presence. "Aren't these good?" she asks him, her cornflower robe revealing her white throat and the top of her gown. "Maybe we'll have these every day when you move in." She looks at me and smiles the smile of those who want only happy endings.

"Anything would be an improvement over boarding-house fare." He has cleaned his plate. "You have some more of these things?"

"One more." A little batter which can be thinned.

"Any orange juice?"

"We finished it before you came."

He apologizes. "I'm ordering like I was at a restaurant. This is more than I expected for appearing like this. I would have settled for a cup of coffee that wasn't heavy duty retread."

"Well, I'd better get ready." Hannah stands. "Eugene is picking me up early today." With dignity she pulls her robe together and tells Ben to come back to see us whenever he is able to.

"What happened to your promise to come by my office?"

"I honestly meant to. But it isn't exactly on my way anywhere. But I really will soon."

"If I'm going to make an honest woman of your mother we better get better acquainted."

Hannah blushes. "You know I don't mean to pester you about it, Ben, but you know that I would like for you to give me away. You don't have to talk about it until you want to." Only her need for this respectability overcomes her reticence.

"You can count on it. I even have a father-of-the-bride tuxedo put on layaway."

The two of them look as if it were all arranged.

I remind them, "That's a long time off."

"I said he didn't have to talk about it now." Hannah looks reproved.

Ben tells her, "Your mother and my lawyer move at the same speed."

She is not sure how to respond to us. "I'll just be a minute if he comes," she says uncertainly.

Ben asks when we are alone, "Are you waiting for me to ask your father for your hand?"

"I'm in the custody of my daughter."

"Then there's no problem."

"Tell me something I don't know," as Roy would say.

We linger at the table like any couple; he drains his coffee, I begin to stack the plates.

"Why did you stop by? You have a class, don't you?"

His earnest face wrinkles in concentration. "My folks used to have oatmeal every day of the world for breakfast."

"We had toasted light bread except when there was enough company for biscuits."

We study one another before I ask, "What did you have when you were married?"

He looks at the used dishes. "I woke up this morning and I couldn't remember. Not one breakfast out of fourteen years."

"Do you want a hot cup?"

"You'll be late for old Henry."

"Old Henry is in New York, remember."

"I cut my class. Fuck the Maoris."

"Was that the class assignment?"

"Every day."

At the door, as he is leaving, he says, "This is a good house."

Reality out the office window is a blue strip of sky that means a good weekend for all the scheduled fun that needs a clear day: the tennis tournament and the Baylor-Texas football game, as well as those that will welcome a stiff wind from the south: the kite-flying contest, the sailboat regatta.

Ben would like to pursue such leisuretime activities of the culture, to crew for a race, to serve in a doubles match, just as he plunges again toward marriage, even though he had no success at it, because it is an assumed part of the weekend scene for a forty-four-year-old man.

Yet this morning he seemed as frightened as I am, and why shouldn't he be: marriage includes so many invariables that you forget about, such as 365 breakfasts a year and rear heavy-duty shocks for the car.

When I was going with Charlie, my first love, and thinking of marriage, which seemed to be a part then of necking in the front seat of a car, it wasn't breakfasts that were on my mind.

Charlie came along when I was trying to please my sisters and shed what they called my "liberal" look, by which they meant needlessly, purposefully unattractive—such as the serviceable shoes and the horn-rimmed glasses. When I met Charlie, everyone at home, even Mother, was as pleased with me as they were ever going to get, which gave me a lot of confidence, and Charlie, as is his style, fell right in with the mood and asked me out, me, in Mildred's hand-me-down cashmere, an early bubble hairdo and the batting eyes that came from trying to see without those glasses.

Charlie and I spent over a year doubling in a parked car, with the people in the front seat watching the couple in the back in the rear-view mirror and everyone hearing everyone breathing, and everyone careful not to spill their cherry Cokes. We spent almost a year like that with his hand under my sweater or up my skirt with him saying, "Oh, honey, Bev," "God, Bev, honey," "Honey, oh, Bev, please," "Please, honey, Bev, God."

It was my first experience with a verbal relationship and I could hear his intonations, his inflections in my sleep. A lot of it I never understood: if he really wanted to pry open my knees, to get to the hairy mound under my panties, what were we doing all the time doubling with his friends? If what he wanted was what he pleaded that he wanted, why did we go on all those blanket parties where couples necked in the grass side by side in a row down the hill from the beer kegs?

During the time we went together we were a part of his group of buddies and their dates. Therefore I was part of the group of girls who sat around and talked together out on the dock, or on the grass in the afternoon if the boys were getting up a softball game. There were often ten of us, going around together only because of who we were going with, a female auxiliary for Charlie and his friends.

We passed the time over Cokes and Dr. Peppers, waiting until the boys came to have a beer, talking about had we ever tried Tampax and if it hurt or if it was easy, which didn't have to do solely with if you were a virgin, and about the curse of having "the curse." I mostly kept my mouth shut. I had never worn a Tampax, and besides, I liked bleeding; it verified to me as nothing from home had done that I was truly female. I could not imagine these girls not liking that unexpected red stain running down their legs that boys spend their junior high years straining to glimpse. Nothing had been finer than the first time I could tell Charlie, "I can't go swimming at the lake Saturday," and see him get it through his head the wondrous secret I was telling him.

I loved bleeding in the first months of marriage, too. It seemed such a womanly thing to say to the CPA, "I can't tonight," as if he were actually ready to go to it every night but for my condition. As if that would have interfered if he had been. There was no more private confirmation of my sex than to fish out that diaphragm with two fingers and find it a little cup of uterine blood, as if making love had called forth the ultimate from my female body (a rite which has disappeared in the era of the pill).

When the girls weren't talking about the curse or if chocolate really makes your skin break out or about a new sweater set dyed to match a skirt, they were talking about how far you should let a boy go. But here I kept my mouth shut, too, because it seemed to me that you and a boy could do whatever you wanted to and that if you ever got your clothes off it shouldn't be part of some game whose rules had been made up by the girls.

There is no doubt that Charlie was the most educational part of my first two years at the university. He did a lot for me. Principally, he plunged me into a group of boys and girls of the kind I had envied and never been a part of in high school, and gave me the chance to see that this was because I didn't belong there.

So it was with only minimal regret that I watched him move on to my sister. Although, in the beginning, when he first brought Dorothy in with that melted look around her eyes and the smeared, kissed look around her mouth, and her blouse all pulled loose and wrinkled, I had to die at the thought of him saying: "Oh, Dorothy, honey, God, please."

After Mildred had graduated and Dorothy had come to school and taken Charlie, there was a time in my life that reminded me again of my year in the sixth grade. For one thing, I studied. For another, the future appeared dependent on my own doing and no one else's. I started a major in English and finished up in Sociology, because that sounded as though it might lead to something important. Again I signed my papers Bananas Foster, in memory of Miss Fordyce, but as all my classes had me listed Foster, B., there was no relationship which sprang to life because of it this time.

Had there been a job waiting or even a vision of a job waiting, the CPA might never have been allowed to take me to wife. Going out into the world alone at that time, in 1956, conjured up a picture of making your life's journey, as Miss Fordyce had done, from Edroy to Sally, Texas. Or in my case perhaps from Sally to Alice, Texas.

Roger, the CPA, told me daily in the coffee shop of the union where we courted that he wanted to be a participant in life, not an observer. That was fine. It was no secret that I had long felt myself an observer as I had neither shot immies on a sandy vacant lot with the boys nor had my shirt pulled up like other girls behind the lockers in the gym. Had I been asked I might have done both. For another thing, I was descended from a long line of spectators, as Opal lived her life through all our dates and our clothes and our weight problems and our behavior. To me to be a participant, then, meant to live your own life and I was for that. Roger could be the one to show me how.

All the countersigns were there; I did not know how to read them. Roger took snapshots of our picnics at the lake so we could see that we, too, were beer-drinking, fun-loving college students. He shouted and grew red in the face for the football team, kept a graph of downs and yardage, knew all the statistics of the Southwest Conference, insisted that after two hours of frenzy, with voices hoarse, we had been participants in the game.

Thinking my future set and a new way of life beginning, as well as still hoping to please my mother—that futile longing you never outgrow—I let myself take a ring from, undress with, and marry Roger Landrum. I took a way out; he took a wife it turned out he didn't want.

Roger had the idea that passion, once the ring was on, could not wait, or rather, that if we were feeling as we should, sex should precede the marriage ceremony. Therefore, once we had gone to visit our parents and told them the happy news, Roger borrowed a friend's apartment and we locked the door and took off our clothes.

That still seems to me the real true event, that undressing, although of course in time we did do what we had come to do. I had never seen a man without his clothes; Mother implied that Kermit was born dressed and would die that way. Roger was white, and hairless in ways I did not expect, and, as he was scared also, looked, when he pulled down his boxer shorts, all too much like the pictures in the high school health books. I had expected our nakedness to inflame me in a way that fumbling in the car with him had not, instead it made me embarrassed for my own body whose breasts seemed smaller out of a bra and sweater and whose belly curved slightly outward above the peach fuzz below. And then Roger—and this is what I don't forget—looked away when I stepped out of my panties.

Roger was the ultimate voyeur of life whether he was watching the teams batter one another or watching the tassels rotate on the silicone breasts at the girlie show. In his own bed he could only falter before exposure. In time he subscribed to *Playboy* to help his marriage bed, and, better yet, found another girl to marry who, when the lights were out, covered herself with nylon and perfume and teased him into leaving money under her pillow. Or so I invented the tale when he told me we were through. In fact he said he had found a really warm girl, a real participant, a girl who wasn't dissatisfied to be a man's full-time wife. A girl who wasn't off carrying placards on the street.

I put his camera in the driveway and backed over it with the car and mailed him the smashed pieces. Of course

I didn't, but I should have. Might have, except that he got custody of the car and the camera.

It is hard to be sure now what was the fault of our personalities and what was the fault of the system's expectations.

At any rate, after Hannah came, things got steadily worse. I spent what seemed to me all my waking hours to make my daughter the person I had never been, to mold the diapered wide-faced child into a girl who could make it in junior high and make it with all the boys like Charlie. To this end I read all the progressive child care books, and did all the usual clumsy things. At the same time, Roger was using the baby also, to prove that he was a successful father.

Many more scenes come to mind that I wish to see again, but one at random will do: a typical Saturday, when Hannah was two. She is in front of the TV watching Biggie Rat and Itchy Brother while I hurry to fry chicken and roll homemade chocolate chip cookies and try to iron some slacks and roll my hair and get out a tablecloth that can go on the ground and make the bed and hang out the wet towels and load the washer, all for an outing promised by Roger. And then it takes us two hours to pack and repack the car and Hannah cries and wets her pants and the food gets cold and Roger explodes.

His version of the same, always substantiated with snapshots, was see what a fun time the three of us had on our picnic in the park. Look how the baby is laughing.

Later his version was that he had a wife who was forever getting wrapped up in what was happening to the cantaloupe pickers, while her own house was a disaster and her own husband never had his shirts ironed or a decent meal on the table.

When he took off, or rather, Hannah and I moved out, I was more than ripe for Meg's favorite comment: Some of my best friends are men, but would you want your daughter to marry one?

Meg and I were friends, although I'm not sure we would be by Hannah's standards. Meg was a big woman, younger even than I was, with one of those broad faces that looks much stronger than it feels. She had broad shoulders, too, and big, chapped hands, which she made jokes about, "I scare them away with my dishpan hands." But that was not what it was: she scared herself because she wanted to grow and live and get the hell away; she could not care too much what happened to the men who came around. And that was a hard way to be in those years.

We would sit at the table and talk for hours about what would we do if we could do anything and who we would be and what we would look like. All the asking that allows you to want to be different or to do things a different way.

She wanted lots of kids and a big old house some days and then she never wanted to have kids and she wanted to quit her job and be a painter. Huge canvases as big as the whole wall. Huge canvases that would go for five hundred or more.

It was the first time someone had said that there wasn't just one right way to do things, the way I wasn't doing it. It was a communion that I never managed with my own sisters.

She pointed out things that were new to me and things that were true. She said, "It's really strange. It's new or something. But nowadays it seems like every time I get together with someone and we have one drink one of us says, 'How come you're staying with him?'" She did not approve of the way I was bringing up Hannah, who was then, while I went jobhunting, going to a day-care nursery school and worrying about getting her hands dirty with the fingerpaints. "Let her alone, Foster. Give her a break. You want to like her when she grows up, don't you?"

When I took the HEXPOP job and Hannah and I could afford to move out, Meg sold her ancient house and moved on. We promised to write every week and never to marry, except for the truest of love, and never to write lies to one another. She must have taken our ice cream freezer as a souvenir; we gave the wine cooler away.

After the first year or two we were down to Christmas cards. What is there to say across miles: you either write *help* or you write *hang on* or you write *I'm making it*, and we wrote all of that, but as we never told our ordinary news, there became less and less to tell.

I'm married she wrote four years ago, *and it's okay*. Next year I might be writing the same to her.

In the years between Roger and Ben there were maybe three men in bed and a lot of daydreams about a dozen others. When you live alone, after your daughter is fed and the dishes are washed and so is your hair and the latest stack of back reading in your field is done, it is a long time until morning. Miss Fordyce must have dreamed of half her students and all of her principals (or all of her students and half of her principals)—people she would not waste her time on in the daytime.

When you are primarily a mother and you don't really want to get to know a man better because you know that would be to like him less and less, sex is a help. It reminds you that you can still respond as a woman, and, in return, you can reassure him that he is far from over the hill. It is not for orgasms that people huddle together in musty rooms under wrinkled sheets, it is for reassurance, in gratitude. It is a need for human warmth that urges you to reach out and fondle and excite parts of a man when you have no desire to cherish all of him. In this way we sometimes helped each other out, and made it possible for each to live alone.

I was ready to love Van's daddy the first time he took me to supper. For one thing I had seen him reappear regularly on back-to-school nights, which showed a reliable character; if he showed up every year to shake the hand of every teacher, then surely he could be counted on not to fade away some troublesome afternoon. For another, there seemed such a strong inviolable part of him that would be Ben no matter how much aging he or the world fell heir to. Looking at him across a hamburger steak, I felt that it wouldn't matter if he got flatulence and hardening of the arteries and had to put his teeth in a glass of Polident, and belched after meals and wore dirty socks and had dandruff and couldn't hold his liquor. He would still be there and he would still be Ben.

Those things mattered, and the fact that from the first time we went to bed he couldn't wait to get to it, to get out of his clothes, already ready to go, to get me out of mine, blinking in pleasure at what he saw and making a grab for it. He loved everything about what he was doing at the time . . . a real participant at last.

He must have felt somewhat the same. He said to me later, in delight, "You just threw off your clothes like it was the most natural thing in the world."

We had not had this before we had each other. He had lived for years with games we have never talked about, games with a strange and troubled girl who never grew into a woman or a real mother. Whatever sex he had had after his wife went in, his emotional investment had a dreamy, frustrated quality. He had for a year or more mooned after a certain rounded girl who sat every morning by the Coke machine in the courtyard of the main building, staring at blackbirds and poking peanuts in her mouth. All year he took his coffee with this student and looked at her and talked to her and tried to touch her here and there, and, then one day, when she did not appear at the appointed time, frantic, he tracked her down to the dorm where she lived, and found out from her roommate that she had transferred to Barnard.

It may be that he never knew more than her name, that she represented for him whatever image of female his wife had once, that he has to have that symbol before him, like a muse or a grace beckoning to him. At any rate, he has never expected me to supply that. He has never projected on me what I cannot be. He likes undressing Foster and does not seem to wish for Beverly without her glasses in her cashmere.

Ben is an anthropologist of the sort who seems more like a psychologist: his favorite studies have been of real Americans in their natural habitat. A former student of Jules Henry, he can give minute attention and attach significant importance to what food people serve and what they say to each other and how they use the rooms in their house. When we met he was directing a graduate project on the behavior, as it related to puberty and fathers, of middle-class white males in the fifth grade in the Southwest.

This drew me to him, as this dealt with matters which are important. What drew us together also was the fact that he was not free and therefore we could not put pressure on one another to marry. He had set the seven-year wait, seeing it symbolically much as the trials in myths and legends. It was a safe period he guaranteed himself.

It is only as it came to a close and we moved into Hannah's house, that he has begun to act like any worker ready to come home with his lunch pail at the end of the day. If now that the lawyer has filed he gets cold feet, thinks again of the safe remoteness of the girl by the Coke machine as opposed to the reality of daily breakfast, I am the first to understand. Ben, Ben . . . did you really have oatmeal every morning of your boyhood?

A visitor to the office intervenes. Just as well; there is no point in reliving the males in one's life. To do a thorough job of that would be to start back with one's daddy. And by the time he got to me he had learned to limit his sociable ways to the drugstore.

The loud woman from the welfare department today wears a kelly green bonded pantsuit with a matching kelly green scarf. She finds that Henry is not only not at his desk but that he is in the big city.

"He'll be back in the morning."

"You people are the hardest in the world to track down. I've left messages for you and messages with his wife who acts like I was after him. It's clear she doesn't understand professional relationships. If you people aren't interested in working out a mutual trade of clients just tell me if I am wasting my time." She gives me her card. "Tell him to call, but I can't be expected to be at my office all the time."

The card reveals what I should have guessed, that she is Clarice Watson, that the visitor from welfare is my fictitious friend. "I'll tell him." And, with the opportunity before me, dressed in a violent shade of green, I do not even offer her a cup of office coffee.

Not wanting to drive home, I take lunch up the street at a counter shop that gives me a bacon, lettuce, and tomato sandwich. "One BLT, out." The waitress, an older woman, offers today a few comments, for my ears alone, on the well-known proclivities of men. When Henry is along, for this is where we go if business overlaps his need for food, she keeps her views to herself, only making inquiries after his general health and commenting on the inconvenience of the weather. Today she tells me that I wouldn't believe the passes men make, married men, right over this very counter.

But then she admits—after she adjusts her girdle so that the bulk of her figure shoves out the top of her uniform and she pushes at her teased red hair and reminds me that if her husband the bird colonel had lived she wouldn't be in this place now—that, wouldn't you know it, it is always the ones you don't want.

I enjoy my lunch with her and do not hurry back to answer Henry's phone.

After a supper eaten to the sound of the news and the sight of Hannah patting her mouth with a napkin, she remembers some news of her own. "Mother?" she gets my attention from the local weather map with its movable cloud cover. "Ben was so nice to ask me again this morning that I really did go by his office."

"He liked that." My response is always what she expects to hear.

Diffidently she tells me about her visit. "He was so sweet about you and everything. And he even took me to lunch."

"Lunch? Where did you go?" Did he do for my daughter the ceremony of lining up the pudding cups?

"He took me to this hamburger place, way up the drag, where all the kids eat, and the place was so mobbed we had to share a booth with two other people. And all the kids knew who he was, or some of them, anyway, and this girl who's the chaplain at the house asked me later how come I got to eat with him, and I told her he was going to marry my mother." She smiles at me. "And he bought me two orders of french fries. I was kind of embarrassed to be such a pig, but I didn't want to hurt his feelings." She says it all in a soft rush, wanting it to be all right with her mother.

"He likes to watch girls eat."

"He walked me all the way back and said to come by any time I wanted to."

"That was good that you went by."

"I told him you were usually busy at noon." Half-way a question.

"Right. Clarice came by and we went up by the capitol for a sandwich and got caught up on our news with Henry gone."

She is relieved. "Do you want me to do the dishes for you? Eugene isn't coming by until eight-thirty because it's his grandmother's birthday and I don't have a lot of homework." She stands in the doorway, wanting things to be fine.

"No, go on and get ready."

It bothers me that she is nervous telling me about her lunch with Ben. It bothers me more that I am bothered by her lunch. It bothers me that Ben was free for lunch today and did not pick up the phone and call. He must have looked up, delighted, to find my nubile daughter waiting hesitantly in the doorway. What more natural for Ben than to feed her?

This must happen with other students, who wait, flushed of face, very young, for a chance to make the one comment they were scared to make in class. To tell the professor that just the other day they were reading a book that brought up the very thing he talked about that morning. Or waiting just to see if they can get a response from the serious, distracted father figure with thinning hair. Lunch with students is his business: I who eat with Roy don't ask Ben for an accounting.

And yet as Hannah talked, the dull twinge of possession that is a side effect of cohabitation reappeared. As long as men stay in their place and only commute to yours, surely such symptoms of the disease of marriage can be avoided.

"Mother," Hannah calls back down the stairs, "do we have any clean towels? I mean, if they're in the washing machine I would be glad to get them and fold them."

7. Family Present

After much consideration, Hannah has decided to miss the Texas versus the Aggies football game in favor of going with me to her Aunt Mildred's for Thanksgiving dinner.

Eugene had drawn good seats for the game and his mother had invited her for an early buffet before the game, but, after talking to me about it over and over, while rolling her hair and doing her nails and opening and closing her biology book, and after talking to Jenny Sue at the house and on the phone, she concluded that a nice girl would be with her own, warm, close-knit family on special days such as Thanksgiving and Christmas, at least until she married into a new family which has its own customs. She told him, "Let me call your mother and tell her myself, because she has been the sweetest thing to include me. She really has. But I know she'll understand that it's a tradition, really, I mean we always go down to Aunt Mildred's, you know, and our whole family will be expecting me."

The drive to Mildred's is pleasant, traveling as it does a more inland path parallel to the old familiar route to Sally. Similarly we go down through German settlements, the Czech farmland dotted with the spires of Catholic churches, past fields that once grew grain and cotton and now grow oil wells, through a sprinkling of small towns marked by signs giving their female names and modest populations.

Gradually, as the sun climbs to midmorning, Guernseys give way to Gertrudis and the land gets drier and lower, until we are into the vast stretches of scrub-oak ranch land owned by the hundreds of acres by a few families who made their money on cattle before they found oil.

Henry my supervisor and I have talked through the years about families, families like ours, that is, not families like the ones who own this great grazing stretch of Texas. As his children have been disappointments to him—boys he says who can't tell their right feet from their left, who, like him, don't know any more about the working of the automobile than the horse it replaced—he spends a lot of time blaming his parents for all of it as well as for the existence of his brothers and sisters, of whom there are over half a dozen, which accounts in part for his interest in population control, as he is the eldest.

His theory is that most of the damage parents do they

do when they are trying their damndest to do their best by you. My theory is that they do the most damage when they are insisting you all love one another. We mull these ideas over when the coffee is hot and his stomach isn't acting up and there isn't a lot to do.

The point being that it is for Kermit and Opal who won't even be there of course because of Daddy's faithful back, that Hannah and I as well as Dorothy and Charlie and their four, are making this drive to spend a day and night together with Mildred and hers, when, meeting as strangers, we might not have a word to say, so that we can each write to Mother to tell her that we all once again got together as daughters of the same union to speak well of our parents. At least my sisters will both write. And Mildred is so dutiful she will doubtless also send part of the feast, a pumpkin cake, or a banana loaf, to Mother and Daddy for their holiday.

Henry, who has made the decision to skip all his family gatherings, only sends cards at Christmas. But when he hears secondhand about his clan's annual Fourth of July picnic and Labor Day barbecue he goes into a great decline and says again that we should all be orphans. On one thing Henry and I agree: there is no getting away from your family.

"What are you thinking about, Mother?" Hannah opens her eyes and turns to talk.

"Henry."

"Mr. Moore? Oh." She laughs a little, with a slight uneasiness, as this does not fit into her view of things. "Will you be needing some gas in a little bit?"

"Doubtless. You want a bathroom?"

"In a little bit." She crosses her legs as she did as a child; Hannah does not want to be demanding.

I come out of the other life I share to look at highway signs. We are farther than I thought and could stop for early lunch, but then we would arrive at my sister's late and full.

"Mother?"

"What, honey?"

"Do you think Aunt Mildred will like my hair this way?"

"Of course she will." Hannah seems to me, with her legs crossed, her air undemanding, gentle, expectant (the same whether waiting for a filling-station restroom or a life with Eugene) to have brought her hair forth from within, a tangible display in its thickness, shine, and mass, of blooming conforming girlhood.

Hannah's hair is my contribution to the kin on this day of general thanksgiving.

"Eugene said," she tells me happily as we pull into a gas station and she smooths her skirts before exposing herself to the service attendants, "that this was the last Texas-Aggie game that we would ever be apart."

Everyone has arrived, and the eight children are being herded as far as possible from the TV screen.

"Sister, if you could," Mildred says to Dorothy, "just tell them to stay out back until I call. There is all that equipment and Dick put some apple juice out to tide them over while we have a drink."

Milk punch is served around the Turkey Day game, and two old ladies who are not Dick's mother and who smell softly of mothballs, hover empty-handed, hoping for some port as in the old days.

Dick takes time out from the game to greet me with a cheek kiss and to pump my hand. He knows just how to deal with me because he is vitally interested in the population problem. In fact, both he and Mildred are continually involved in matters of community concern.

Dick was consulted at the beginning of Project Salt Vault, concerning where to dispose of atomic wastes from nuclear power plants. He made many suggestions and warnings on bedding them in Kansas salt flats; he predicted possible explosions due to small intra-crystalline brine inclusions. I know because he sends the family all his timely monographs on engineered storage.

Mildred volunteers many hours of her time each week to the immediate crises in Texas. For example she was a forerunner in heralding the threat of VEE (Venezuelan equine encephalomyelitis), which broke out in eight South Texas counties and killed and sickened over three thousand horses; she fears that the dread African swine fever of Cuba will be carried into Mexico and across the border; some years ago she was vitally concerned with the eradication of the screwworm. She is the only person to have been twice awarded her area's Outstanding Woman of the Year plaque.

Today Dick and I agree that if the birth rate does not abate the world will soon be formicating with human beings. He tells me in consternation about an article he read which called concern such as ours alarmist, which said that if people had made the same interpolations from the number of horses in the days before the automobile as we make now about population they would have predicted that today the whole world would be knee-deep in horse manure. I file the story away for Henry and accept a milk punch. We agree that sort of attitude does not help our cause.

Mildred joins us. "Sister," she says, "we never forget that all our concerns are secondary to yours. Dick and I often say, don't we, Dick, that ours is the last generation to be able to allow itself the luxury of four children."

If I were to put myself inside Mildred, in a gesture of empathy, it seems to me that a sudden tightness would set in, a constriction of my larynx, my pyloric sphincter, my bowels. The blood vessels of my head would clench like fists as I made sure my four school children were headed with certainty to the eastern universities of Dick's choice. In bed I could manage only the rigid scissoring of long, thin legs . . .

It must be somewhat that way for her as twice already since we got here she has pressed firm fingers to her forty-four-year-old temples. Between her eyes are two deep lines that look as if the glare of living is too bright.

Although Mildred was continually vexed with me when we were growing up, she was very helpful to me. She was more definite than Dorothy or my mother. All matters were clear to her so she could make it clear to me that one did not cling to warm radiators in hotel rooms or shriek out with nightmares in the middle of the night when others were trying to sleep.

"You are nice to have us," I tell her. "Can I help?"

She lets me follow her to the back where she says, "Well, it's all done except last-minute things like putting around the tea." With some satisfaction she shows off the tables, set with burnt-orange linens and gold glasses, with a large bronze mum centerpiece on each; in the kitchen she displays three ducks baked in an orange glaze, and, waiting in the freezer for dessert, liquered orange ice in scooped-out scalloped orange halves for those who might find her pumpkin pie with whipped cream too heavy or too customary. Platters and trays and casseroles and wine bottles await the signal from the men that they can turn their attention from football to feasting.

Mildred always has a color theme, an additional arbitrary stress she places upon herself. When she did Christmas for us last we had a banquet of red and green: cold gazpacho, baked salmon with snow peas, raspberry sherbet with crème de menthe.

"It's all beautiful. You have outdone yourself."

"Sister," she lowers her voice, "you could do me one favor, if you wouldn't mind. If you could sit in the kitchen with Dick's great-aunts? They are going deaf and it is such a trial to him. We've put the four youngest children in there, too, away from Dick's mother. He does so want to show Hannah off to her."

"Old ladies and I get on." All of us who know our place.

"You really would be dear to do that, Bev."

"Let me know when you want to set the tea around."

Over our feast, the two elderly women on each side of me do their best, which is not nearly good enough for this household. The one on my left cannot see what she is eating and keeps asking over and over for the cranberry sauce, of which there is none, to go with her turkey, which is in fact duck. The other, on my right, cannot hear and keeps shouting questions at the younger nephews and nieces who bicker endlessly and make fun of her.

From the other room Hannah's gentle voice says, "Yes, ma'am." Above the other voices and the sound of silverware on plates, I hear her say, "Oh, that's so sweet of you Aunt Mildred, do you really like it?" She compliments the dinner before her. "This is the most wonderful meal I've ever eaten." She flourishes surrounded by the manners and speech of those so like Eugene's mother.

It is worth these family meals with Charlie for me to hear her say to the matriarch, "Oh, yes, ma'am, we always do," in a voice that is not ashamed of whatever it is that she insists we do. She is not hindered by me; it reinforces for me that none of what it took to create Hannah-spelled-backward was in vain.

Content, I assist my friends in the kitchen. To my left I serve orange relish onto duck slices and call it cranberry with turkey; to my right I turn an old wrinkled face around so she can see me mouth the words, "Have a roll?" without intruding my voice into the next room. I kick, beneath the table, a nephew.

Foster, who does the dishes at home, offers to do them here.

"That would be really great, Bev. And I could get off my feet a minute if his mother will let me. But do be careful with those dishes of hers. Leave the good plates if you want to and I'll tend to them later."

"Is Dorothy with the children?"

"Hardly. She can't handle her own let alone eight. Did you see those children of hers at the table, the way they behaved? But of course you did, how stupid of me, you ate with her younger two. And mine probably were no better, I admit. Anyway, I sent them into the back yard with Hannah to ride herd on them."

"She'll enjoy that."

"She's a love."

"Thanks for sending her the dress material again. She sews something new for Eugene at least once a week."

"She's so lovely, sister, I can't believe it."

"She takes after her aunts."

She smiles slightly. "I didn't mean it like that, Bev." She presses her fingers to her temples. "But think what it must be like not to have to work at everything, to wake up every day with that fantastic figure and all that hair."

"Like Dorothy."

"Like she had. Poor Dot. She must have gained ten pounds with each of those children. It doesn't take much to see that Charlie is already wandering. He has eyed everyone but the aunts."

To change the subject, I ask, "How are your headaches?"

"The doctor has about decided that they are not true migraines. He has tried to take me off sugar and alcohol and coffee, but who can live like that and go anywhere. He has put me on some medicine that means I can't have cheese, can you imagine. But, they're some better." She gathers herself together to go back into the fray, having forgotten she was going to put her feet up.

There is no dishwasher. The sink is the old-fashioned double kind, very deep, with dish drainers on rubber mats beside it. A sink that assumes continual kitchen help. My arms in soapy water, I can see the children play out the window. The two sets of cousins run around Hannah like around a maypole. Dorothy's three girls and Mildred's one gaze at Hannah as if wishing hard enough would transform them with their thin legs and short hair into her. The two youngest boys who ate dinner with me are digging behind a clump of bushes and it may be they are burying a playmate. Mildred's bigger boys are above this whole gathering and have changed into their white tennis clothes. It is impossible to imagine how one could relate to so many egos as dependents, or how one could follow the paths of each. Those of us who have one child must do so because we know our limitations.

And, of course, because we had a choice. The thought of being pregnant year after year, in bondage to the CPA and stuck in that mistake because there was no way out, makes me almost break a good china cup.

"If she calls me 'sister' one more time, I'll scream." Dorothy finds me sudsing and lets off steam. Mildred is her nemesis. "Honestly, I know it's her house, but the way she orders everyone around. You shouldn't be out here all by yourself doing this, Bev. She can afford it, she should have got some help to come in. I bet she has ten Mexicans a day to do what you're doing."

"Do you think Mother and Daddy wish they were here?"

She giggles. "We ought to offer all to come to their house for Christmas. Mother always talks about how wonderful it all was at Grandmother's house at Christmas with that rich boiled custard that only Mildred pretends to remember."

"You shouldn't have to do Christmas if you're doing Hannah's wedding. Tell us all to go stuff our own turkey."

"You know I love to have you and besides you know that all you get at my place is canned peas and brown 'n' serve rolls." She makes a face at the remains of Mildred's lavish meal.

"We have a house now." Would they come to Hannah's?

"Forget it, Bev, you're working and we're not. Besides you have to go where at least half of the little kids are. Imagine them all running up and down your stairs in that beautiful room."

"I've been watching them out the window."

"Dottie really looks up to Hannah, you know?"

Dottie ought to be looking up to her own mother who has such charity for all of us. Dorothy is in a loose blue dress the color of her eyes and her cheeks are red with impatience at her eldest sister. She looks as she did as a small girl when Mildred used to straighten up her box of paper dolls.

"I'll finish up," she offers.

"If you'll stack these, I'll take some tea and rescue the aunts."

She giggles. "They sure enjoyed their wine, didn't they?"

The aunt who doesn't hear too well is delighted when she sees me wave, and she follows me out onto the porch, away from the rehash of football conversations which she can't follow. She can talk just fine, however, and takes this opportunity to unload the burden she has carried with her: they are robbing her blind at the rest home. In fact, not only have they taken the counterpane which her own grandmother crocheted and a photograph of her mother in a gold frame, but they have stolen Papa's diamond ring that she has had in her glove box for safekeeping since he passed on thirty years ago this very month. Things aren't how they should be since she moved into the retirement home with her sister.

Out in the cool sunshine the smell of mothballs has been transformed into the smell of lavender or wisteria, a purple smell of dried leaves. Tears roll down her cheeks as she tells me her story and I hold her soft wrinkled hand in mine and nod my head at each new disclosure.

How can one go on when Papa's diamond is not in its velvet box?

Across the road from us are rows of grapefruit trees as far as the eye can see. I wonder in what direction lies the stretch of acres of irrigated soil that belongs to our old enemy, Sabrosa. Somehow the valley that is Mildred's is such a distance from the valley that belonged to the melon pickers.

"She's catching her death of cold," Charlie says through the screen door, knowing she can't hear a word.

"There are worse things to die from."

He lets himself out onto the porch and pulls up another rocking chair. "Getting up in years."

"Her or me?"

"What's that?" The aunt leans toward the youngish man.

"Hear you're still working, Bev."

"Still." It was the personal way he used to abbreviate my name that prompted me to change it permanently to Foster.

"What's it like?"

"HEXPOP?" I know he doesn't care.

"Being a career girl. All the nurses I know can't wait till they can get pregnant and quit."

"I thought all nurses were in love with their doctors."

"I wish." He has flesh under his eyes that sag and a jowly look I associate with too much liquor. His former way of staring at you with his eyes half closed as though he wanted to rip off your clothes, has declined to the practiced stare of a man used to handling and undressing bodies. The novelty of exposure has worn off; now he seems to be sunk in the general habit of asking all the women who come along, out of habit.

"Do you like your practice?" And I don't care.

"Sure I do. Makes lots of money." He doesn't pursue it. "I get over your way once in a while," he says, leaning across the lavender lady between us. "I might give you a call."

"We're all getting married at my house." No need for Charlie to waste himself in my direction just to stay in practice.

"You don't say?" He lids his reddish eyes. "Bev's got a beau."

Beau: what a foppish word. I answer him in kind, out of some other southern era where he still lives, "I'm keeping company with a professor named Ben Roberts."

"Good for you." He pushes out of his rocking chair. "You're going to catch your death of cold out here," he shouts in my friend's deaf ear.

"What's that?" she says.

What the shit, he seems to say as he opens the screen door and bangs it behind him, you offer them what they want and then they don't want it.

I am ashamed to have said that to Charlie, to have bragged that Ben is offering me a marriage. The point of living together is not to keep away men you knew in college. Where is the Foster who should have looked old Charlie in the eye and said: The prof's so good in bed you needn't bother.

"I'm sorry about the ring," I tell the aunt, touching her empty finger so she will understand.

"They stole it: I know it." She gazes vaguely across the lawn, beginning to shiver in the wind.

When I help her through the screen door my fingers find little between her loose flesh and her bones.

Mildred and I surprise one another in the kitchen at midnight.

"Sister," she says, startled, "what are you doing up?"

"Same as you, not sleeping." But now I fix a glass of instant tea. I came down earlier, barefoot in my cotton gown, to slip out on the porch to see if I could hear the grapefruit growing, but heard instead only the sounds of heavy trucks hauling in the night. The valley is still part of the past for me, populated as it is with farm workers and plantation owners and acres of citrus fruit.

"Let's finish the wine, then," Mildred says, almost gaily. "It can't make my head hurt any worse." She sets out a half-full bottle and two Mexican glasses which are irregular, colorful and much cheaper than those we used at our company meal. "Tea will keep you awake anyway." She pours for us. "I can never sleep any more. As soon as they are all down and Dick begins to snore, I am wide awake. When three of them were in diapers I used to think I got up because the house was quiet and I could have it to myself. Now that they are all in school, it's gotten to be a habit. As my doctor says, I have conditioned myself to expect it."

In old habit we settle ourselves on each side of her wide wooden kitchen table. We drink an unspoken toast to the best times at our parents' house, when Daddy spread the evening paper out on the table, and read aloud the news in the tone of voice of some of the rednecks who hung around his drugstore, and Mother cleared up the dishes while listening to her favorite crooners on the radio. There weren't many times when we heard our daddy's sociable voice, nor many times when Mother was more interested in something else than in what we were saying. We loosen up a little at the memory.

We don't say anything important; I am careful not to intrude into Mildred's life. Sisters are difficult kin; too close to deal as strangers yet with not enough in common to be friends. We, for example, have between us only Daddy at the kitchen table and Mother at the sink. But for a change we make personal talk; no HEXPOP, no VEE.

Taking the pins from her streaked upswept hair, she brushes it down to her shoulders. "Are you still dating the anthropologist?"

"He's filed for a divorce from his wife."

"That's grand . . . then you two will get married?"

"He says so."

"I thought you might never again." She shakes out her hair. "Do you ever hear from Roger?"

"He sends a yearly Christmas card with his son's picture."

"He always was a creep. That must be hard for Hannah. Does he ever see her?"

"She still writes to him. She doesn't want to lose a daddy. But he doesn't answer. She told him she was getting married—not a line."

"She does want a real family, doesn't she? It was touching the way she played up to Dick's mother." She puts her hair carefully back into its twist and presses her fingers to her temples. "Sometimes," she says, "it's like my head was in a vise and I think if I don't get away . . . I know it's my own fault. Other people don't wear themselves this ragged. At least that's what my doctor says. He says I have to learn to condition myself to do only half a job."

"Dick said you were taking a trip?"

"I don't mean a vacation, I mean away where I don't have to carry it all on my shoulders any more. Yes, we're going to Vail again this year to ski. In two weeks." She gestures to indicate the burden of such chores as shopping for after-ski clothes, lining up carpools, doubling her exercises, arranging a hairdo that will keep. Then she lays her hands flat on the table, as if to will her whole being to be calm and still.

"Let me rub your neck."

"No—it's fine." Back in character she gets up and pulls her robe about her. My offer to touch was out of order.

"Then get some sleep." I rinse our glasses.

"You, too, sister. You can't wander around in that sheer nightgown with this many people in the house. For goodness sake, let me lend you a bathrobe."

On the steps in the morning sun we take our leave. While Hannah talks to Mildred, I discuss with Dick the article in *Foreign Affairs* on the heat-trapping effect implicit in increasing populations. He demonstrates he understands fully the principle of physics involved and shares the fear that we will suffocate ourselves early in the next century.

"He said, Aunt Mildred, that this would be the last Texas-Aggie game we would ever spend apart."

"He's a lucky fellow, Hannah. You tell him I said so. Maybe we'll get to meet him over Christmas."

"It sure was a wonderful dinner, the best I ever ate."

"You were a love to look after the little ones." She pats her niece. "Don't forget I want to give you your wedding reception, champagne and all, something really special that will set that small town of Dorothy's on its ear. We'll carve your faces out of ice, or write your names two feet high in carnations. Something. Now don't forget."

"Well," Hannah demurs happily, "that would be really sweet of you to do that."

"Take care, Bev," my sister says to me, as I am now only another relative on her way home, and not a favorite one at that.

"I forgot to ask you last night: what happened to Papa's ring?"

"Oh, that poor pathetic thing. She gave you the whole story, I bet."

"The counterpane and her mother's picture."

"They are all like that. They accuse one another. The other aunt breaks things and then the rest home has to call us and we have to pay the damage."

"Where *is* the ring?"

"In Dick's lockbox, I guess. Most of their valuables are."

"Well, thanks for having us. Good-by, Dick."

"Did you see," Mildred concludes, "those kids of Doro-thy's over breakfast?"

Getting into the car, I have a new insight into kinfolks. What the mothy, lavender aunt meant by "they" stealing her blind was not the ladies at the retirement home.

"Wasn't that wonderful?" Hannah is buckled into her seat belt, turning the pages of a magazine. Her mind is on the big, warm, family Thanksgiving dinner. "It must be wonderful having sisters. I mean sometimes I imagine that

Jenny Sue is my sister and if we had lived at the same house all the time we were growing up that would have been really special."

"Mildred was a big help to me growing up." We are back in the giant rolling ranch lands, orange groves far behind.

"What did she do?"

"One time she told me to go back to sleep; one time she gave me a used sweater."

A hurt silence descends on Hannah, who studies the pages of her magazine with great attention. Her face is pale; if she has to go to the bathroom again, here in this one-horse town with one open station and a Coke machine, she will go to her grave before admitting it.

"I wasn't near as nice to Dorothy." That young girl with white straight legs like large pale canned asparagus stalks.

But Hannah is no longer picking up on my sister stories; as the city limit sign goes by she crosses her legs silently.

After a few miles I explain, "I gave her Charlie."

"*Mother.*"

"Let's stop at the next town, honey, and get a hamburger. If there is a next town. We ought to get out of this stretch someday."

Still no answer, but an hour later as we pull into one of the small towns with girls' names, she says in a patient voice. "I guess it's hard on you, isn't it, Mother, seeing Uncle Charlie even after all this time. If it was Eugene and Jenny Sue or something I guess I'd die. I know you used to go with him; Aunt Mildred told me."

"That was before he met Dorothy. It was all over by then." I dismiss the topic. "They got engaged her sophomore year, just the same as you did."

"She told me." Hannah blushes, pleased to have emulated Dorothy. "But you got married right away, too, didn't you?" She does not want a rejected mother.

"The same year." To hedge the facts somewhat.

Hesitantly, she says, "I saw him come out on the porch to talk to you."

"Oh, we're old friends by now. I only brought it up because Dorothy is such a peach of a person."

"She really is, isn't she?" Reassured that her mother has said something straight-out nice at last, she celebrates after we find a bathroom by having a milkshake and french fries for lunch.

On the drive in I meditate that mothers and daughters have it even harder than sisters: they never please one another.

8. Family Past

December is affable. There is a cool nip in the air to hurry Christmas shoppers, a few gusts of north wind to blow at the Salvation Army captain ringing his bell, but the days are still bright and clear. It is holiday weather, crisper and drier than football weather, but still two months away from winter.

Hannah is with Eugene constantly now that finals are over. Tonight it is another eggnog party or an open house, for which she has spent the afternoon sewing a floor-length velvet skirt.

The ironing board is set up in the corner of the dining room by the table which holds our small pile of toys and presents for Dorothy's children.

"Oh, Mother, it's so exciting I can hardly believe it." Hannah comes in, radiant, in a pink, long-sleeved blouse and the sweetheart-red skirt.

Does she refer to the party they are going to, the new outfit, the way her freshly washed hair fluffs about her shoulders, or the prospect of Christmas Eve at Aunt Dorothy's? It is hard to tell. Tentatively I respond, "You look lovely."

"I mean, he really sounded like he w-wanted to. That it wasn't just something he was thinking he had a responsibility to do."

Oh, yes.

"Do you think I ought to write and tell him what all will be going on and everything? Like he asked?" She is so pleased, so anxious to please.

"He can't come to Dorothy's. He can go to the rehearsal dinner; Eugene's mother can talk to him. He can come to the reception; the country club under Mildred's firm hand will hold both of us. He can't come to Dorothy's. All right?"

"Well, I can hardly just come right out and say something like that to Daddy in a letter. I'm sure that he will know what is the discreet thing to do anyway. He has been around a whole lot, you know." Ever so slightly she raises her chin in defense of her father.

In customary style the CPA has saved his bombshell for the back of his yearly Christmas card, which shows all of them beaming in front of their large house. In similar fashion in other years we heard of his marriage, his move to Arkansas, his prize son.

He wrote Hannah:

". . . will naturally plan to be the one to give away my one and only daughter in marriage. Am sure the young man is to be highly congratulated on his taste. Send me details of my duties when you have them and such extras as the engagement notice from the paper, a formal invitation, and such, so that we can begin to share the festivities in advance. Although I am sure you have contracted for a professional society photographer, some of the most memorable shots will doubtless be taken by yours truly and I shall count on that. Is it still the fashion in Texas to see who can produce the most bridesmaids? My wife joins me . . ."

It is so like Roger to appear. Naturally he will be trim, graying, and handsome, his big white hairless body in a well-tailored suit.

We got the news in the mail today, and Ben, who has gone for the holidays to his parents' house where Van, Jr., will not join him, as she has gone to Chicago with her artist friend, does not yet know that even if he hustles along and changes my name, he won't be father-of-the-bride. In one way, at least, Roger's coming will take the pressure off; however much it will give me such things as headaches, heartburn, and irritation.

I burn my thumb on the iron as I diligently spread out a blouse of Hannah's. "Tell him whatever you want, honey. We will all be civilized." There must be some reason that people who have lived together once agree to behave in public as circumspectly as the English at tea. It must be for the beholders. Left to ourselves, some of us who are divorced might prefer to be uncivilized.

"It's so exciting. I can't wait to tell Eugene and Jenny Sue. It is like a dream come true." She pats at her hair. "You be sure to leave me these gifts for the kids. You know I love to wrap them, and especially Dottie's, because I want hers to look real grown-up. She's at that age. I want them to look really pretty. Do you remember last year how Aunt Dorothy had pink angels and red balls and red ribbons everywhere, and all those branches and holly? It was the most Christmasy thing I ever saw. Maybe," she says shyly, "I can do our apartment like that next year. She said some of the angels on the mantel were built around hair-spray cans."

Eugene's arrival puts a stop to all this. "We won't be late, Mother." Hannah promises.

"Take your time." I burn my thumb again. Irons and I have never got on well.

"Ben won't mind will he, Mother? I mean he can still walk down the aisle behind you and sit by you and everything. He will surely understand because he's the father of a daughter himself, you know." She struggles to remember her old classmate, Van.

Carefully I apply spray starch to a sleeve. "He'll understand."

As she leaves on Eugene's arm she calls back, "You be sure and let us know if we need to take you to pick up the car when we get home." Smiling in the doorway, she adds, "Maybe next year Ben will be taking care of your oil leaks for you, Mother."

This blouse of hers seems to have a multitude of sleeves, as when I iron one side of a sleeve and turn it to press the other side, the first side wrinkles again. This blouse is the skybaby blue one that goes with a skirt, and also, well co-ordinated as her wardrobe is, a pair of plaid pants with cuffs. A heavy metal triangle hot enough to burn flesh seems a poor instrument for readying garments. We should go back, or forward, to washing them on stones in the river and smoothing them to dry in the sun. Soon, a hundred years or so, if we are still here, we can wear paper and recycle it at the plant. This iron then will go in a historical museum. At least it does not have graduated holes which spit steam like the one Mother had.

I can hear her voice, "Beverly, you got that dress soaking wet. Don't you even know how to use an iron?"

A voice at my elbow says, "Don't stop the good work."

"Roy." I set the iron down. "You startled me. Why didn't you knock?"

"Who knocks? I could tell you were burning something."

"Get some iced tea and sit down. Hannah's gone."

"Brought us a Lone Star beer." He divides it and straddles a chair in the dining room. "Where's your car?"

"Getting a new hose for what I hope is all that is causing this oil leak."

"Head gasket."

"Don't have any ideas that cost money."

"You ever get shocks?"

"Sears did that for me."

"I could of done that." He messes with the bay windows but discovers that they are just to let in light and do not open. "Where you been eating? You haven't been home. The prof been feeding you?"

"Sometimes. Mostly I've been eating up the street from work to save time."

"Sure." He seems older and harder in the weeks since

he's been around, more set in non-success. If you don't like your family and you don't have any money, Christmas is at the top of the list of bad times.

"There's meat loaf left. And some chocolate cookies she made."

"Not right now." He watches me fumble awhile. "Where you getting ready to go?"

"To my sister's for Christmas."

"You went down there Thanksgiving."

"Other sister."

"This the pushy one?"

"This is the one who did the party here for Hannah."

"Oh, her. The florist." He thinks about that. "She taking her sweet-boy up there?"

"They're saving that for next year."

"Types like that aren't in any hurry for anything you can name."

Hannah's blouse is adequately dewrinkled. With some relief I put it on a hanger. "Whatever they do, they're out doing it."

"Not much, you want to bet?" He spins his chair around with two legs off the floor like he was popping the front end of a motorcycle. "You doing her clothes for her, aren't you?"

That doesn't need an answer.

"My mom does that. She works all day in that crummy store and then wears herself out trying to keep my sister dressed like she thinks the big-shots dress."

"Like the cheerleaders."

"She *is* a cheerleader, what do you think? That's the whole point. Don't you know what girls like my sister do while us ropers are all out screwing our cars? Didn't they teach you anything down there in that one-horse town you come from?"

"Not much."

"She likes all that family stuff." He is back to Hannah. "She likes to go to Dorothy's church on Christmas Eve."

"Yeah. Christians are the only ones who can afford Christmas."

There is a blouse that looks like heavy satin with a tie at the neck that must be to wear to church. Most of these things that Hannah sews are synthetics that need a very cool iron, as I have learned the hard way on a favorite dress.

Roy gets up. "Let's go get your car. I'll run you up. I'm tired of sitting here."

"It may not be ready. The man said he'd call, but he was really behind because of everyone going out of town."

"What time did you take it?"

"Five-thirty."

"It's ready if it's ever going to be." He shoves his chair under the table. "You never rode in my new car, did you?"

"No." But I do remember a good ride in his old car. What a nice car that was. I borrowed it once, on our old street, and was entranced with the smell of grease, plastic, and stale cigarettes, very fragrant. It reminded me of cars in Sally that I never got to ride in, cars with missing hubcaps, busted radiators, dented fenders, the kind that showed steady use. Where the back seat once was, in Roy's car, was a gaping trough with two or three jacks, an old spare, a few untouched schoolbooks, a disintegrating blanket, a paperback porno, and a wool sweater his mother must have searched for everywhere.

His new blue Mustang revs up its rpms and takes us down the street, giving a very smooth ride. My hair is still damp, as I do not get it fancy for Dorothy, and the wind whips it about my face. There is something about the clean vinyl seats, the radio blaring away, and the manner in which Roy keeps adjusting the rear-view mirror that reminds me of double-dating. All that is missing is the cherry Cokes.

"Do you take girls out in this car?"

"There's no shortage." He tightens up, like he's been condescended to.

It was a question that anyone with tact or brothers would know not to ask. I look out the window at the night lights as we whiz along the residential streets twenty miles over the speed limit.

At the second stop light a lot of cars honk at each other, hands wave out the windows. The kids, paired and packed into the cars, look as though they are on their way to park, bumper to bumper, on some dark hill overlooking the lake. Group necking, shades of Charlie.

"Creeps." Roy speeds past them. They are not his crowd, or rather, he is not their crowd. It can't be by choice that he is running errands with Hannah's mother on the first night of the holidays.

I try to cheer him up. "You're driving like we were in a stock-car race."

"You scared?" He doesn't mind that.

"I think there're cops behind every tree."

"They're saving their strength for longhairs. They're only interested in the other kind of speed. Those cops, they don't care if we have a smashup at every corner." He takes a sharp curve. "When girls do that," he says, as

I hug the door handle, "I reach across like I was gonna open the door and say, 'You wanta walk?' That usually puts an end to that."

Impressed, I take my hand away and roll with the turns.

At the service station my plain vanilla Plymouth is waiting in the row of finished cars. There is no dark stain seeping onto the concrete beneath it, at least. Cars have so many ways of getting to you.

"Hop out," Roy says, swinging open my door across me. "I'll meet you back at your house."

"You don't need to."

"Didn't get my chocolate cookies."

Roy and his life remind me of my days of trying to make it out of Sally, Texas.

There aren't many roads out of a town with 5,280 people, a population figure kept constant on the city limits sign despite census fluctuations, just as the town proper was kept at a mile square, even when houses grew out past it in all directions, so that at such public events as the annual area jamboree it could say on our town's sign:

SALLY, TEXAS
POP. 5280
ONE SQUARE MILE OF FRIENDLY PEOPLE

Sally is one of the many towns in the region named as if for girls one has known only casually: it is north of Violet, east of Alice, west of Olivia, south of Bonnie, and shares its valley with the sister town of Celia. In its beginning its location seemed to promise a booming future:

it is nestled between two rivers, straddles the Southern Pacific railroad line, is part of the Coastal Bend area which reaches to Corpus Christi.

When I think only of the town itself and not about my family in particular, it is easy to get the homesickness and the nostalgia that you feel for those imaginary places, like rolling blackland farms with pigs, that you invent for your past.

Nowhere on earth seems to my memory as flat as just outside of Sally where the edges of the horizon in all directions wave into a steamy watery mirage that reflects the grasshoppers pumping oil and the old wood farm-houses and the fields of new green sorghum shoots.

And there is nothing in my life since that has replaced the news items of its weekly gazette called the Sally *Sentinel*. First-page news, complete with staff photo, might be that Mary Svoboda defeated Amando Ybarra for first place in the spelling bee, with the paper noting that "she spelled the winning words 'lambent' and 'lieutenant' to defeat her opponent." A small-town sociable tone of voice was used for all items, whatever their lurid content. Thus, on page three, it might be reported that "Ramon Hinojosa, a visitor to our fair city, sustained injuries about the face and neck due to a twelve-gauge shotgun, while engaged in an alfresco affray at the family home of his brother Guadalupe Hinojosa."

There were the good do-nothing times in Sally that are a large part of the life of any small town—fooling around after school along the railroad tracks, jumping from tie to tie, racing to the nearest crossing; there was the game of putting your ear to the steel rail to hear if a train was coming.

One time my sisters and I all climbed into an empty boxcar and switched dresses. It was a very daring adventure, to be where we had no business being, to undress outside our house, down to our panties. Even Mildred was dared into it and was a lookout for us while we changed. We shared with each other the gossip that all children ten and over heard at school. We told different versions of the story of the man in town who went to the steakhouse up the road where he was to get fixed up with a girl, and it turned out to be his own teen-aged daughter, and we all knew, or thought we did, who they were.

Sally bloomed twice, once when they brought in the railroad and again when the oil company began to produce in the fields to the north. All the buildings in town are distinguishable as railroad landmarks or as new modern oil improvements. The county courthouse, with its benches of snoozing old men in hats, is the best example of railroad days and has a historical marker by the door. The new Savings association, all glass and brick, went up in the oil boom. When the oil money came in and the company town was built, Daddy moved his drugstore to a new building across from the Church of Christ, the dry-goods store put up new striped awnings, and the town installed its first parking meters.

The company town was built to house its employees in fine style, which included a company swimming pool, out beyond the town proper, just past the double row of palm trees and salt cedar that had once marked the city limits. When the houses were built with their wide-screened porches on the front, looking much like the rows of officers' houses at Fort Sam Houston, the townspeople felt immediately alienated.

The company porches were clearly places for their inhabitants to sit and have an alcoholic drink and take the breeze safe from the coastal mosquitoes. All of the town houses had their screened porches on the back where they belonged: a porch was a service area for an old icebox and the Maytag washer. Also all the town houses, on their flat curbless lots, had yards dressed with oleander bushes and banana plants, and small fancy flower gardens. The company people on the other hand were satisfied with the mesquite and salt cedar just as they grew.

It was with satisfaction that the town people noted in recent years that the company town, like the old S.P. depot in Sally, and the MoPac depot in Celia, looked like the remains of an abandoned camp of a defeated southern army, and that what oil crews now came in lived as transients, in trailer parks to the north.

In its heyday, Daddy's drugstore had been a social gathering place for men from in and around the town. His new store had such niceties as a special seasonal table in the center, dividing the pharmacy from the fountain, which displayed treats such as heart-shaped Valentine boxes of chocolates with soft centers. But the conversation was the same as it had always been.

Dad liked to listen to his old friends, farmers like Vlasak, who came to town to talk about the threat of downy mildew to the grain sorghum and the advisability of trying Fasgro 131 and the idea of caterpillar control through using papernest wasps, and what the going price of anhydrous ammonia was. That kind of talk was about the life he had moved to town and gone into the drug business and helped send his younger brother to pharmacy school to get away from. He liked to be reminded of his escape.

His daddy had been in vegetables instead of grain and cotton; he had operated shipping sheds for beans, squash, okra, onions, and cabbage. But despite the ready labor force of Mexicans like his fine foreman Rudy Cavazos, there was no way to second-guess the weather or the variability of the market or the disposition of the ducks and jackdaws that pecked up the crops. Such conversations reminded Dad he would never have to watch his crops being plowed under as his dad had. Besides, as the men agreed, it was no use to work your back bent growing crops, when your neighbor like as not was going to buy a Piper Cub with the oil leases on his back forty acres.

His ears ever open to word of trouble, Daddy was one of the first to say that the oil was going to peter out and he was leaving before it did. Which, with all of us out of school and gone, he did. He took his nest egg and the secretary-treasurer of the Ladies' Auxilary to the Volunteer Fire Department, and moved to the metropolis of Corpus Christi, away from the daily ag news about the county agent and the migrant worker and the failing company town.

Mother didn't mind the move, because things are lush and green in Corpus and visitors from home oh and ah over the seacoast and she has her sister there who married well, which gives each of them someone to tell about the upward mobility of their daughters. Besides, Mother gets mentioned in the *Sentinel* as a visitor to our city from Corpus Christi every time she comes back even for a bridge party, and that makes up for the anonymity of the large, humid city.

I can enjoy these memories of Sally; it is when I get

down to the actualities of my own family that things grow less pleasant.

The story was that Daddy and Uncle Chester had had discord even before Daddy's back operation. Which must be true as I remember constant exchanges between them in the back of the drugstore.

Uncle Chester would say that he was the only one who knew what the no-good help was up to, that Daddy was given to keeping on any shiftless worker who appeared. "That's who makes the money in this world, Kermit, them as don't work. I told that boy, I said, 'You get off your goddamn ass and go to work or you get your goddamn ass out of here.' Now you try to tell me he's staying right where he is?"

Then Daddy would overrule Chester because he owned the store. "He isn't real fast, I know that. He's what you'd call slow. But he comes regular as a clock ever since the morning he was late and I told him, I said, 'You didn't get here on time this morning, Johnny, why don't you go home and try it again tomorrow.' You take off a day's pay and they start hollering like their tail was in a crack, but he's been regular from then on. First thing when I open the door, he's here."

Whenever he wanted to end a discussion with Chester, Daddy said that men were divided into those who picked up hitchhikers and those who didn't. That Uncle Chester didn't because he didn't trust anybody; that Daddy did because he and his dad had met lots of hard-working, down-and-out boys in their time and had given them a chance.

When Dad moved to Corpus, Uncle Chester said he would not go along because the whole town of Sally would die if the pharmacist left, as he was the only one in town who knew the first thing about medicine, the doctor not knowing "his ass from his elbow."

In Mother's family, Grandmother fought with everyone too. Although in later years, as she began to die a long, tedious death, she acquired the matter-of-fact view of things that I remember. As she told me about her maid, "She has these seizures, but they're not to worry over. It was the result of a train-car wreck and not her fault. She's not young but neither am I. You get one who doesn't steal, you make do." She liked to run down my grandfather whenever his name came up, then conclude by saying that it was good riddance, and that she had provided for herself better than he did anyway. Her relationship with life was much as she described it with this long-gone husband: "We got along no better and no worse than the average."

My mother yearned above all else not to be what her mother had been, a nobody. She intended to be socially noticed, to get her picture in the paper, to have friends who would compliment her often. Because she didn't have much else except us to use, we were the means by which she tried to get the world's attention. But when you live vicariously, you don't receive enough of life, and therefore nothing we ever did was enough for Mother, not even Mildred with all her talents, nor Dorothy with all her charms, and certainly not Beverly.

Miss Fordyce served to show that there were ways to live for yourself. Born in Edroy, educated in Kingsville, with a brother in Corpus, she has lived her whole life in three counties. She elected not to marry, in part, I guessed, because she did not want to change her name, a fine name which was somehow touched with oil; in larger part she did not marry because she did not want to change herself. To us she insisted every day of our year in her room: you have to do something important with your life.

She expected more of us than we were used to giving. What we kept in our heads was our business, as what she had in her desk drawer was hers, but we were held strictly accountable for the words we spoke and most particularly for the ones we wrote down. What an uphill fight for a woman to insist on a weekly vocabulary test in Sally, Texas, when the winners got no mention in the *Sentinel.*

The one other person who had visions of something important in Sally was Aunt Gladys, the Sunday school teacher who was Chester's wife, but I had a blind spot about her because I saw her filtered through Mother's eyes. She did two things the family could not forgive: the first was that she let her hair go iron gray in her thirties and the second was that she never wore any lipstick, which was anathema to Mother.

Aunt Gladys told me once that if she really had the courage of her convictions she would help those kids who didn't speak English to make something out of themselves.

I said, "You could teach, like Miss Fordyce."

"Your Miss Fordyce only helps people like you, child, who don't need it. To do any good you need to get them at three years old. There ought to be public nursery schools." She had a vision that it took the government twenty more years to get.

Later, in college, when I understood this better, I challenged her when I was home on a visit about why she had never tried to set up that kind of program for the migrant children.

Her answer was, "Well, I have to think of Chester first. He don't want me working. It wouldn't do to be embarrassing to him when he's trying to serve this community. Besides, I have my house to run. I do what I can, child, on Sundays, in our Methodist nursery."

The other thing Gladys did that was unforgivable was to die suddenly in her sleep with no fanfare. She was found with a small frown on her ashen face. Grandmother had led us all to believe that death gives plenty of warning and allows for much hindsight into one's life. Aunt Glad did not even permit her husband to issue the ritual sheaf of prescriptions that was his due as a pharmacist, a sheaf such as accompanied the former occupant of our yellow house out the door of mortality. Mother considered the death, as she had the lack of lipstick, as the hostile act of a stubborn woman.

It might have got me out of Sally sooner if I had listened to all Aunt Gladys had to say.

But although I am neither Miss Fordyce nor Aunt Glad to the boy who waits for me in my driveway, his car door open, his radio playing, at least I provide a place to share a beer.

Roy and I give up on the dining room. With our window open over the table-shelf, we get a strong dark December wind, which blows the last moisture from my hair. It smells almost like frost. Surely the right sort of night for going down a rocky mountain path to Bethlehem. Once in Sally they had a live crèche at the Lutheran church with loose chickens and sheep wandering around and an old jersey cow who made a patty by the straw. A nice pregnant farm girl was Mary. It was the most believable Christmas I can remember.

"You look like a hippie with your hair like that." Roy watches as I comb out the tangles. He is restless.

"What's on your mind?"

"I quit school."

"What happened?"

"Nothing new. I was busting out anyway. What was the point of making an F plus just for coming to class?"

"What did your mother say?"

"Mom screamed at me for an hour that I'm as good as dead without an education. Then she called community college and told them they'd better not drop me if they know what's good for them. Then she followed me around half of last night proving that I had plenty of time to study if I wanted to. She said that because last night I finished off a few six-packs with some guys. I don't study because I don't want to. Sure I can figure out what they're talking about out there, but I can't figure out why."

"What did you tell her?"

"I promised her I'd start over in the fall if she'd get off my back about it. She tells me at least once a day, no school, no future. Her idea of future. She thinks if I really work my butt off I can even get a job someday with the fucking telephone company."

"Will you go back?"

"By fall I may be chipping ice in Alaska." He fiddles with his empty glass. "But as long as she believes it, that's the main thing."

It is easy to understand his mother; if you have been

kept down, if your husband was kept down for not having schooling, you don't care what jobs there are for mechanics who can fix oil leaks in cars like mine. You've got your tired eyes on thirty years from now. "Roy, what do you want to do?"

"When you types ask that you always mean how am I going to make money. If you didn't you'd just ask me what I want to do Saturday night."

"I mean with your life."

"You mean how do I want to make money." He sees that he is right, and he has more to get off his chest. "It's different for girls. Look at her. All a good-looking girl has to do is get married. She could bust every course and it wouldn't matter a damn."

"That only puts the problem off, getting married."

"Yeah, you tried that, didn't you?"

"So did your mother."

"I said good-looking."

I ask the question he wants instead, "What do you want to do Saturday night?"

"Ball, what else."

I smile, not able to fault that. We give in and eat the last of Hannah's cookies and add our trash to the growing stack.

"Be seeing you," he says.

"Will you be all right?"

"Same to you."

It is hard to see him leave with none of his future resolved, in part because it is very much my future, too. When Roy stops revving his motor and stealing hubcaps and settles for life into a job that stains his hands and grays his neck and clouds his eyes, we will all be lessened by it.

"Thanks for taking me to get the car."

"What do *you* want to do Saturday night?" he asks, from the back door, his jacket zipped up.

"Ball, what else?" I smile to use his phrase.

"Oh, *Mother*—" Hannah and Eugene stand, shocked, in the doorway from the dining room.

"I sure fuck things up, don't I?" Roy says lightly. "Good evening, Eu-gene. Long time, no see." He goes over and holds out his hand.

Hannah tries her manners, falling back on them automatically in her distress. "Eugene, you know Roy Hawkins." She is miserable, her cheeks white, her eyes full of tears.

"You're the one who drives around campus all the time looking for us, aren't you?" Eugene has not taken the hand, he does not heed Hannah's introduction. The brown-eyed boy shows with his whole clean-shaven face that he does not like this dropout. Eugene has the air of a young boy who has seen a dog run over and stops his car to move it from the street and rings doorbells to try to find its owner. He didn't hit the dog, but he is there and he isn't evading his responsibility.

"Must be someone else, I've got better things to do." Roy slouches against the door, eying them both. Satisfied to have got this scene at last.

"You d-did so, Roy." Hannah accuses him. "You drove past the fountain again last week and kept honking and staring at us. You know you did."

"Must have been someone else. I got more to do than watch sorority girls bat their eyes and show it off. Your mother and I were just talking about what else we got to do."

Hannah turns scarlet with shame and lifts her hand to strike his face. She is innocence brought to this in her very own home.

But Eugene prevents her. "Don't waste your time on him. He was just leaving." Eugene, still in his overcoat, takes Roy by the collar of his leather jacket and propels him out the door. We hear him say, "It won't be necessary for you to show up at this house again."

"Anything you say, sweet boy."

"The next time you come around we'll get out the police."

"Don't trouble yourself."

Eugene comforts Hannah, and cools her flaming cheeks with his slow hands. He expresses his faith in her over and over while I stand numbly in the way, finally rinsing plates and glasses.

"When we're married," he vows, "this will never happen."

"Oh, Eugene, you were so good to throw him out."

"There wasn't anything else to do that I could see."

"Roy has always made trouble for me."

"He won't make trouble again; I'll see to that. He won't ever make trouble when you move out of here." He looks at me over her shoulder and there is no dishonesty in those direct brown eyes; he is not evading that he is forced to place the blame on me.

After Eugene has gone Hannah starts to cry. "Oh, Mother, how could you talk like that with that awful Roy? How could you let a person like that come around?"

"Roy isn't a criminal element. He fixed this shelf, this table for me, remember? And the fence around the garbage cans." Who else saw that I was without a place to put my elbows and read the paper; who else cared that my pantry overflowed with garbage? Who around here deals with me about reality? "He's a boy you used to date, Hannah."

"He has embarrassed me so bad I can never face Eugene or his family again and you are on his side. You honestly don't see anything wrong, do you?"

"I think he wanted to talk to you again. You represent something to him, something he had and lost."

"Roy Hawkins never had any part of me, Mother." Her face is red and angry.

"He needed someplace to let off steam. He's dropped out of school and his mom of course is upset."

"You let him come here and eat lunch, too, don't you?"

"He is welcome to eat a peanut butter sandwich here. You've had lunch with Ben. This isn't all that different."

"Oh, Mother, this isn't the same at all and you know it." She goes into the dining room to wipe her eyes and pull herself together. I see her going through the unironed stack of clothes. In a very tight voice she says, "I'll finish pressing up these things you didn't do, Mother, if you'll do the dishes. We'll have to wrap the presents early in the morning."

Wordlessly she sprinkles and irons her nice clean holiday clothes.

I bring her some cold tea.

"Everything was s-so exciting."

"Eugene knows it wasn't your fault."

"You didn't even see—" Tears run down her face as

she shows me the long-awaited symbol of her betrothal. "He gave me my r-ring."

There is the diamond of splendid caratage that Eugene has placed in a proper setting on her long white finger. He presented it, she tells me, in his formal front room (while Foster was letting her hair blow dry in a blue Mustang), in the presence of his mother, who wanted to share in the surprise. It was given tonight so she would have it to take to the traditional close family gathering at Aunt Dorothy's. "This is the last Christmas we will ever spend apart, darling," Eugene surely said as he sealed it with a kiss.

"How can I ever look him in the face again?"

"You can, that's how. He will forget the whole thing; it made him feel good sticking up for you. Now come on. Tomorrow is Christmas Eve."

Hannah's wet eyes look at me steadily. "I won't forget," she says. "I never will."

Three: Hannah and Foster

9. An Open House

"Come on, let's go get a beer. My treat. We need to make hay while the sun shines."

At a Mexican restaurant three blocks from HEXPOP, Henry and I settle into a deep plastic booth over a pitcher of dark beer. We are trying to absorb the impact of the Supreme Court's seven-to-two decision to leave the question of abortion at the discretion of the woman involved.

Henry wants to give an all day picnic on the ground, to put the big pot in the little pot, to use his favorite country expressions, to celebrate abortion and to honor the twenty-seven-year-old lawyer who argued the winning Supreme Court case. "She's a real landmark; you've got to hand her that. She deserves more than your passing recognition. It's up to us to put on a show for her. And it certainly won't hurt us either."

"Some kind of open house?" The second glass of tap beer is warming my feet, getting me in the mood for celebration.

"A memorable event, that's what. We've got to pull our own weight, Foster. When I was at national you wouldn't believe how lots of offices don't do anything but hand out the standard leaflets. Lots of outfits don't talk to anybody but the saved. This is our big chance to break new ground."

There are lots of options. We could have it at our office which would be good publicity, during working hours, with some sort of awards ceremony presenting her with a plaque. We could give a luncheon at which our lawyer could deliver a speech to such staff people as our welfare contact, Clarice, and others of her ilk with clients to refer. But Henry leans toward a nighttime affair in the German beer garden, a pleasant setting that would let us ask state and local officials of some note and thus be guaranteed coverage by the media.

Considering the gamut of choices requires another pitcher of the frosty draught beer.

"Did you tell Shirley you were going to be late?"

"Did I tell her? You bet your life I told her there was an organizational conference over the high court's decision. If I hadn't called and had failed to show by now, she'd have the police after me."

"Does she get mad if you're late for dinner?"

"Does it get hot in the summer?"

"Why is that? Mother used to bless us out if we kept supper waiting. If we weren't all there when she was ready for us to sit down. And there was nothing to the meals. She had her two good recipes in the auxiliary cookbook and she was forever making her famous biscuits when we had company, but the rest of the time it was what my sister calls a canned-peas supper."

"You're talking about my present-day situation. Shirley must not have anything else to do except figure out how to throw something together that's going to dry out if you're not there on the stroke of six o'clock." He fortifies himself at that thought with another glass of Michelob. "If you've ever done without food, which I don't want to make a sad story out of, but if you've ever done without, you know how good food can taste and you don't go around drying it out. My mother could make cornbread and slab bacon taste like what you pay a restaurant your eight dollars and fifty cents for today." He is back into his Hard Times, which he does not mind discussing, now that there's been the distance of some thirty years. "I don't want to labor my point, but there was more than one time growing up when we lived on sowbelly and grits. We ate grits fried and grits boiled and grits like they were cereal, with a pile of milk and sugar."

In the next room a guitarist warms up a half-lamenting Mexican song. Our dark waitress with a decorated comb in her high hair hovers about as we finish our pitcher of dark.

"Henry," I try to voice my lingering reservations, "we don't want this to be a party. We have to make it clear

175

that this is a way to thank the lawyer for doing what she or someone had to do because we have failed to offer women better alternatives."

"Absolutely. This is a serious, critical matter. But we want to do it up right, with printed invitations, none of your mimeographed stuff, to each and every person on our mailing lists. We've got to have something we're not ashamed to send out to all the bigwigs in the state offices, plus a copy up to old New York herself."

The waitress lights the candle in the old wine bottle on our table: a signal that it has become the dinner hour. Henry, not wanting to appear cheap, instructs her to bring us menus. "My treat," he says.

"What about your canned peas?"

"She'll be asleep if I wait late enough. She can chew me out in the morning over cold eggs. Regular as a clock she takes that sleeping pill at ten o'clock. And she is very literally dead to the world until seven in the morning. Last weekend you remember we had that frog-strangling rain? It leaked all over the bedroom floor and she never knew a thing."

I decide that Hannah can surely feed herself and roll her hair and read her homework, or, if she is going out with good old Eugene, she can leave me a neat, polite note saying that she won't be late. Surely she doesn't need a phone call from her mother, reporting in.

We have full plates of enchiladas, tamales, and guacamole salad, with a side order of chapupas each. The food is blistering hot with fire and jalapeño peppers, and it is a good inspiration for our projected festivity. We decide to serve our guests bowls of tamales along with their paper cups of beer.

"You check with her, will you, and set up a date. And maybe you could design one of those formal invitations that looks like an invite to the governor's mansion. You let me make up the guest list to be sure we cover the entire waterfront. Don't want any local pol to get his nose out of joint."

"What if our lawyer says no?"

"Don't borrow trouble."

It takes a long time to plan a city-wide event on a matter of national importance. Over coffee and pralines we note the fact that it is ten o'clock.

"You think," Henry says, gathering up, "when you get married that you're getting away from your problems but the truth is that home is no different from home, if you follow what I mean."

"Yes. Sometimes I hear myself say to Hannah the very same things I said to my mother." Such as my friend Judy and my friend Clarice. "They both want me to have friends."

"The exact same thing with my present situation. Shirl is always after me to go out with 'the boys,' why don't I go bowling with 'the boys,' or hunting with 'the boys.' She's got these big-time goat-roper brothers who are really into guns."

"Why do they want you to be a group?"

"Beats me. When I get home all I want is a little peace and quiet, not to mention a decent meal, maybe have a beer and watch the ball game. Get my mind off things. Why should I go out to some function? Hell, I know what guys talk about, the same thing they always talk about; why be reminded what I'm missing?"

"Maybe we say the same things to our children that

our parents said to us. Maybe we're passing it on along like pushing over a stack of dominoes."

"That would be a waste of breath at my house, passing on what my old man said. Those kids of mine aren't worth the price we pay their dentists, just for example. They don't have a sense of responsibility. You know what I'm trying to say, Foster, they don't pull their own weight."

Near our building we part ways to get our cars, reassuring each other that the evening has been essential to our cause. The streets are thawed and dry; it seems years since I have been out alone in the dark. It would be pleasant to walk from downtown to the campus and back every evening. Though in this weather it would be more comfortable in jeans and coat with a pull-down knitted hat.

It always seems that Henry and I talk of families and food, but this may be due to the fact that to talk of families is to talk of food. Although now that they are gone no stories of Grandmother or Gladys fail to mention the one's floating boiled custard or the other's grated potato pancakes with hot applesauce, while they were alive we heard only of Grandmother's thick flour gravies that smothered every dish and Aunt Glad's stingy pantry with no spices and little refrigeration. Even Mildred, who has done all those things in the kitchen the others never thought to do, such as handle real dough and learn to taste sauces and whip a mayonnaise slowly from oil and lemon juice, will be remembered as the one whose meals gave her headaches.

It could be that the answer is to get the family out of the kitchen. How solidly Henry's stomach handled the chili peppers; how ravenously I wiped the last bit of cheese sauce from my plate with a rolled-up tortilla. But that may be because we weren't eating with our kin.

The night air is so clear and cold it seems a shame to leave it. I am like a child allowed out past my bedtime; it is with reluctance that I finally pull the car into the gravel driveway.

"Mother, where *were* you?" Hannah waits for me in the lighted doorway in her cornflower blue bathrobe. Her mass of hair is ribboned in matching blue. She is a study in consternation, but consternation wearing clean bedroom slippers and fresh lipstick.

"Henry and I stayed down for supper."

"But you couldn't have been at your office because we called there three times, Mother, and there was no answer."

"We ate at El Gato."

She follows behind me into the kitchen. Her tone is very bothered. "You mean that you and Mr. Moore went out to dinner?"

"Hannah, what is the trouble. Surely you fed yourself?"

She speaks very slowly, "I made a green pepper omelet like we learned last year in cooking class for Ben and me when he came looking for you. He hadn't had anything to eat." She pauses so her news will sink in. "It just seemed like you would have called to let us know. We had no idea where you were."

"I know Ben appreciated the omelet." I pour some hot water on a tea bag and slip out of my shoes. It appears Ben is beginning to drop in for meals. Does he expect to find me waiting in an apron at seven in the morning and and seven at night? Does he want out of a union the very thing Henry and I abjured: a meal that will dry out and get cold if you aren't there on time?

Hannah waits at my elbow, still aggrieved.

"See you in the morning." I disengage myself from this homecoming reception, teacup in hand.

"It seems like you could at least thank me for feeding him while you were out in a public place with *a married man.*"

She prefers a private place? "It's Ben who got fed; he can thank you. He's not my Lhasa apso who can't open his own Pard can." My ears listen for the expected: Oh, Mother.

But instead she turns on her slippered heels and goes out of the room. Things have been different with Hannah since Christmas. If she is still angry with me for talking with Roy in my own kitchen, no doubt she can cling even longer to my indiscretion tonight. Why didn't I just say Henry and I stopped off for a couple of pitchers of dark beer. She might as well be privy to all the facts. Henry at least fared better, having come home to a wife dead to the world, her fury held suspended in a corner of the brain until morning.

Hannah returns to the doorway, composed. "You wouldn't do this if you were married to Ben." It isn't quite a question.

"Eat Mexican food?" When she puts me on the defensive it vexes me too much to gather together the parable of the co-workers and the open house. The idea that marriage means you must be a cook on call has made my tea turn cold. "What did Eugene say about your feeding a man supper in your bathrobe?" Two can play this business.

She flushes, "Ben is going to be my *father*. Eugene certainly can't . . ."

"And if he isn't going to be your father?"

"You're twisting everything in a very distorted way."

"So let's get off this and go to bed. Henry and I have an open house to plan."

"What do you mean what if Ben isn't going to be my father?"

"You've already got one, remember. He's renting a cutaway to ride into town and give you away. Having two fathers would be bigamy." This time the water is boiling when it covers the second tea bag. A nice hot cup in bed and a chance to glance at the afternoon paper would be pleasant enough to make up for this fracas and for missing Ben as well. I am easily lulled by the propect of some sleep.

Hannah stops in the hall, still more on her mind. As she lays a white hand lightly on the bannister rail she looks like the mistress of a large house bidding the servants good night.

If we are to continue this dialogue, as they say in the encounter groups, I must sit down, and I do so on the arm of a chair. "Yes, honey. What is it?"

"Before all this came up, there was something sort of important that Eugene and I had talked about and he has already talked to his mother about . . ."

"All right."

"We were wondering if it would be proper for Daddy to stay at Eugene's house. I mean of course I know he can't stay here, but it seemed like I should offer to put him up somewhere. You can't ask your own father to rent a motel or something."

"What is your hesitation about his being at Eugene's?"

"Well, they do have a guest room which is really pretty, but the thing is that his mother isn't married either, that is, she's widowed and we wondered if it would seem right for them both to be there together."

"Maybe Roger will bring his wife." Maybe I'll appear in public nude and finish off this thing once and for all. Hannah's problems are of a shallowness so defined that even a goldfish might gasp at their level.

"We don't believe he will, Mother." Because that would be awkward.

There is a distance between us that has not been here before. This may be due to my caterwauling; it may be because these marriage preparations have far exceeded my span of attention for them. With great effort I summon my Emily Post. "Eugene must have had boys over to spend the night. It seems to me like you could consider Roger a house guest of the groom."

"What a good idea because he really is here because of the wedding and all. We could even say that in the paper which would make it clear to the people who might not understand."

Hannah Landrum, writes the Sally *Sentinel*, was given in marriage in a lavish ceremony at the church of her aunt, a former resident of our fair city, by her father, who for many years estranged from her mother, was at this time a house guest of the groom. The event in the church was followed by an alfresco buffet in the lovely rose garden . . . "We could indeed. It will be like when

Ben's daughter is here; although she will be in town to see him, she will be officially your house guest."

"You didn't tell me Van was coming for the wedding."

"Not then, on her spring break. That's in about a month."

"You didn't happen to tell me. Is she supposed to stay here? In my room?"

"Somewhere upstairs. Ben told her she could."

"Well, if Ben said that . . . I guess he wants to tell her about his plans with you." She hesitates. Her old school-mate's visit is a problem that she must accept: after all, she and Van will be almost sisters. For now she goes back to the more pressing matter, to be sure she has settled it with me. "We thought it would be a nice thing to go ahead and tell Daddy that I had a place for him to stay. So he would know that I really am counting on him to come."

"Write him. Fine."

She studies me to see if I am being sarcastic, but decides not to press it. With a smile to make up, she climbs the stairs.

In the rollaway it is difficult, rather, it is disheartening, to think at once of weddings and abortions; it seems the better part of wisdom to forget the tea and sleep.

Henry and I have a fine February night for our open house. A crystal evening following ten days of freezing sleet. The great live oaks in our rented German beer garden hang lanterns from branches that last week had icicles. We had feared that by tonight the streets would be impassable and the plane that was to bring the lawyer home from a speech in Kansas City would be grounded;

that we would be forced to have our celebration huddled inside the small frame building around its lone gas heater.

We have worked all afternoon to arrange the benches and decorate the tree-covered fenced yard. As we felt that the smallest hint of Valentine decor would be out of place, we have kept our color scheme to green and white, the colors of life and hope or the colors of spring after winter, or, at the least, an inoffensive early St. Patrick's day. We put some daisies around and set candles in sand in paper bags to line the walkway into the garden, and candles in the lanterns. Just before Henry turns his face into its public smile and readies his hands for officials, legislators, state employees, doctors, lawyers, women in expensive shoes and the media, we make a toast from paper cups.

"Every child a wanted child," Henry proclaims a slogan from his past.

"Beer in every cup."

"Foster," he lowers his voice, "talk to Shirley, will you, for a few minutes, just till I get things set up."

Henry has his wife here but not his sons, as I will have Ben, who will enjoy putting the function in perspective for me later, but not Hannah.

She was dressing for the sweetheart dance when I came home to change. Beautiful red velvet skirt again, this time with the white satin blouse and red carnations from Eugene. "Mother, you understand, don't you, that there is no way we could explain my not being at the Valentine's dance? I mean, how could he say to his mother or the guys at the house that I had gone to something for *abortion?* Besides, it seems like it would create the entirely wrong impression if you had unmarried girls there

184

anyway. You don't want to seem like you're approving of that or anything." She tied a velvet bow in her hair. "I know you and Mr. Moore have worked hard on this" —a slight edge to her low voice—"and I just hope you have everybody there whom you want to come."

Shirley is persuaded to sit on a bench with me out of the way while Henry talks to some TV cameramen who have twenty minutes to give us and can't help it if they are early. She is a narrow-eyed woman easy to dislike, especially when she delivers her shrill voice through that pursed mouth. And, as usual, I give in and dislike her.

"Henry has certainly worked hard to put all this to-gether," I tell her, to pat him on the back.

"So my husband tells me." Emphasizing that it is *her husband.*

"I sure hope we have a good crowd."

"Seems to me you two spent a lot of time on this that didn't need to get spent. The less said about this subject the better if you ask me."

I wave at Ben, who gestures from the gate that the lawyer is arriving, that the evening is beginning. My short dress seems all right; it is a new dress of green wool, but a working dress. My hair is washed by me. This isn't a beauty shop night, this is the night for people who care to come together as they are.

"That your intended over there?" Shirley peers at Ben.

"Yes."

"Glad you two are finally settling down."

"Well, it's not that stage yet . . ."

As Ben and the lawyer join us, Shirl asks, "And what does your gentleman friend think of your going out drinking beer with married men until all hours of the night?"

Henry and I have a few minutes to set our plans with the lawyer before the people begin to come. She mills about among them, mistaken half the time for a house-wife, holding out her firm hand and introducing herself, very low-key. Every one we hoped to see has come, even Clarice in a red-bonded pantsuit with matching scarf, and everyone seems pleased to be outside under the stars with the weather balmy and the beer flowing.

"We really are proud of you," an older black woman says to the lawyer.

"The time was ripe for it." She smiles and gives her hand.

"But it meant so much, you being a woman."

"I did hear someone say at the back of the Court's chamber, 'I don't know who she is, must be one of their secretaries.'"

"We are sure proud—"

And then it is time for her to address a few words to the crowd. Henry and Ben help her up on a bench where she can be seen, a fair quiet woman, no more than a girl, in a long paisley dress. The wind blows her streaming hair and everyone bends to catch her words.

As she talks, the faces of her listeners seem marked by personal experience concerning the world's unwanted children: a man thinks of his teen-aged daughter; a woman of her grandmother who had ten living children, another, younger, of her own sister who died of a hemorrhage at the hands of a quack; a doctor has memories of a battered child; a judge of abandoned children. They want to hear that there is now a way to make the already existing one million annual abortions safer and more sterile, as available to the poor as to the rich.

The lawyer expresses her deep appreciation for all the work that groups like ours have done at the local level to create a public climate which made the court's decision possible. She emphasizes that the decision will be nothing, however, unless the services are made immediately available to all women, that it will be a hard fight to get the hospitals and doctors to follow through with what is needed, and that therefore groups such as HEXPOP must not let down their efforts.

She tells us that the decision left the choice of conception with every woman where it belongs, but says that to make such choices legal is just the beginning, that in time, as we learn fool-proof ways to provide all women with the right not to conceive, abortion will become unnecessary.

At the last she urges the assembled to want for every child food and space in a world which will accord it dignity and worth.

Her words remind me of the inadequacy of the feel-good gestures of our melon-picketing days. For then we had a chance to walk a month in flat, worn shoes from the valley with the farm workers, as well as to work around the clock to guarantee that the governor and the press and those legislators who could effect laws were on hand to meet them when they trudged the final mile up the avenue to the capitol building. But we did neither; instead we had a party to celebrate the cause.

They remind me also of Roy's attitude last week toward this open house: he could not understand how it could be a matter to have a party for. His face was guarded as he explained that it was the worst that could happen to a guy who makes out with a girl, and it was the worst that could happen to a girl who has no money, such as his sister.

"You ever had one?" He asked, his tone flat.

"No."

"My mom did."

"Women will be able to go to a real doctor, to have it in a real hospital."

"Shit, making things legal only makes them more expensive." He had stared out the window at the broken fountain filled with ice, forgetting that he had come to apologize for messing things up with Hannah. "You don't know the first thing about it, since it never happens to *her* kind."

The lawyer reminds me, all of us, that it will not solve any of the remaining problems to stand here and clap for her speech and then go refill our paper cups.

Clarice and another woman listened with me under the big live oak and now Clarice makes a quick introduction, excusing herself for not doing it more thoroughly by saying that it is hard to keep everyone placed in a crowd this size. She tells the other woman that I am "Moore's secretary, over at HEXPOP"; she tells me that the woman "does the legwork for one of those family outfits." Her mind is not here, stuck with other women. She wants to work her way into the group of male doctors gathered by the beer keg. To that end she practices her critique of the lawyer's speech. "You'd think she might have laid down some medical guidelines." And she is off.

The woman and I introduce ourselves better. I tell her Foster is not Henry's secretary, but she understands that and says it must be because I carried in the coffee. She has the same problem. She is a psychiatric social worker. Who pours the coffee. I tell her that I meant years ago to work in a family service agency but that maybe I'm better off not dealing with people like that. She says she had meant in college to be a politician and expose corruption but she found it didn't want to be exposed. We talk about our jobs and then about our families, and in hers, as in mine, she is always identified as the one "who works."

Her name is Alice Jean and I ask if she is married, and then, as she was but isn't, we find ourselves in a very long conversation on divorce as the crowd begins to thin.

"We must tell her good-by," Alice Jean says, seeing that the lawyer is leaving.

"She made me feel guilty."

"She wouldn't mean to."

"But this is our area and what are we really doing?"

We talk about it with the lawyer. That we must use this public recognition to solve the problem of procreation, must use this opportunity to justify the long years of research and education done by people before us.

As we talk what I have been doing seems less important than it did before. What after all is the point of the dog-pound flyer which now seems flippant: only that children may soon be running loose and unclaimed. Such an example offers no solution either to the problem of their birth or to the problem of their survival.

Alice Jean asks her, "Do you think the hospitals will co-operate?" and, "What will we do if they don't?" and, after we have explored that, "Do you think there will be bills before the legislature to put limits on it? And what can we do about that?"

She and the lawyer know all the concrete problems involved in working through the institutions that have to put something like this law into effect. Hesitantly, I offer to write up a draft of some of their ideas in a form that might be mailed around. Something to let women know what might happen next and what they could do on a local level.

The lawyer says she will be in touch with me.

I thank her for coming.

"I hope I said what you wanted to hear." She is modest.

And then Henry takes her away, on his arm, to shake a few remaining hands, some belonging to important people.

Alice Jean says, "Let's have lunch sometime."

"Some place where neither of us pours the coffee."

"Right."

Ben has left to join me later and Shirley is sulking. But Henry and I are in no hurry to put things to bed. We want to rehash our success again from start to finish and we do, all the way back to the cameramen who came too soon and took the wrong shots. We extinguish the votive candles in their paper bags and gather up legions of sticky beer cups littering the ground. We go over what the lawyer said, and what the politicians said, and what a good time was had by all, especially those tireless workers from HEXPOP.

Shirley has decided that something is going on between us and she has attached herself to a student who stayed to help and who now hears all about her boys who are neglected by their father who never wants to do anything but sit in front of the tube until she goes upstairs to sleep.

"We did it, didn't we?" Henry says to me.

"*She* did it."

"The time was ripe for it, which means we all did our part. We did just what your average dedicated, far-seeing community agency would do." He is in good spirits. "You have to hand us that."

"She made it seem right that we got everyone together."

"She has the class all right. But don't forget we had the idea."

A wind has come up from the north which shakes the trees as we take down the lanterns and put each back in its box. "One more toast, Henry." We drain the last of the beer in the last of the cups.

"Here's to the idea," he says.

Shirl has had enough. "As my husband you might have made arrangements to take me home to our children if you were planning to be here all night long."

"Here's to all of us," I say, "for getting one step farther down the road."

"Be here *with* me, Ben."

"I'm here." He moves a leg against mine.

The cold wind gusting against the side of the house seems the fingers of the outside world tapping on my high window pane, reminding me that the world does not go away, even while we make love.

Our open house has taken Ben's mind from those daily matters which irritate him; he enjoyed our party. He is familiar with tribes' attempts to limit fertility by the use of barks, roots, inserted objects, prohibitions, infanticide, taboos; he looks upon the Supreme Court's legalization as a recognition by the chiefs of what the natives have been practicing all along. Naturally in such cases some public ceremony is in order: yams might be roasted in the coals or a flock of doves released into the air. It can as easily be beer beneath an aging live oak.

"That wife of Henry's is something else," he comments.

"She thinks I'm running off with him."

"Don't give that a thought. She uses you as an excuse to chew him out; it if wasn't you it would be the lady at the dry cleaner's."

"Our evening out to plan the open house made trouble all around."

"At least your daughter got worried about you. When mine lived here I could have been missing fourteen days and she would never have looked up."

We have pulled the covers up and it is very cozy. The temptation is to sleep. Ben brought some wine and on top of my bottomless paper cup of beer it has made me very drowsy.

I try to recapture the feeling I had listening to the lawyer talk, but it is late and it is easy to push such thoughts far away. "Didn't you like the lawyer?"

"She's not much older than my students. Gave me the feeling of seeing a flashback in someone's life. There they are interviewing this militant old lady, another Margaret Sanger or Carry Nation, who has put a hairpin in the current machine and brought the state to a grinding halt. There's a closeup as she talks about how she got her start with the landmark abortion case. I guess I don't believe in her as a beautiful girl in her twenties. That sort of woman should have wrinkles if not a hatchet."

"This way she is more like the rest of us."

"The rest of you have cold feet."

Which I think he means literally as mine are on each side of his warm leg. When you really look at what is important, as we did tonight, it sends you hurrying for support and comfort and a place to warm your feet. There has to be some time when it is safe between bouts of grappling with world-wide hunger and the right of each separate woman to her separate womb; a time when you do not want to be separate. "Be *with* me, Ben."

"You can't want it again; you're half asleep. Lie still and I'll warm you up before I have to get out of here. This isn't part of the evening program for Hannah's Valentine social."

10. Another Daughter

We have the few weeks between frost and drought that is spring in Texas. In the brief time after the ice storms, before the baking heat, all the windows in house and car are thrown open and we breathe outside air. Never have the trees seemed so green or the fragile pear blossoms so white; never has the purple mountain laurel been so fragrant.

Students all over the campus are in short-sleeved T shirts and lightweight jeans. They lie in the grass and gaze at each other as we all would like to do all day.

Hannah has withdrawn even more into an area beyond my reach, bringing carefully no news of Jenny Sue or plans for spring Round Up at the university. I attribute this coolness in the midst of spring's lovesick foliage to the fact that Van is here. She and Van are not doing well inhabiting the yellow stucco house. They cannot exchange words, as neither understands the other in the slightest. Van seems to speak in tongues around my daughter, who speaks to her in platitudes.

Tonight there will be four of us, Van and Hannah and their parents, in the dining room with its wide bay windows. Grownups thinking of marriage get their disparate young together.

"The weather never settles down till Easter and Easter is late this year, so don't let this sunshine fool you." The checkout girl at the grocery store explains things to us.

Because of Van we are boycotting meat, to protest its high price. Our grocery basket looks like the wartime rationing days of my childhood, with a few differences: I don't think zucchini and snow peas were invented before the Second World War.

I am not in favor of the meat protest; the only ones who will be hurt are those on the bottom of the ladder, those persons easiest for small packers to fire. But Van's fervor for the boycott reminds me of my melon days; it is a need to do without that I can relate to. For her we had cheese soufflé yesterday, for her tonight we plan egg salad.

I have always had empathy with Van, Jr. It seemed to me when she was in grade school that at the parent-teacher conference the blame for her behavior could justifiably fall on me. There was so little to respond to when told that Hannah was such a model child, so neat and so dependable. Van, at that stage, was neither. She broke her pencil leads, lost her cartridge pens, excelled in mathematics, took up for the one black child, the one fat child, the one poor child, in a school body then as homogenized as mayonnaise. She liked some teachers better than others and some not at all. These fluctuations in behavior concerned the young ladies assigned to process her; these choices set her apart from girls such as mine as far back as the fifth grade, at the beginning of the gathering together into Bebe Lee's and Cheryl's groups. Van, Jr., trying to hang onto herself in the days of public education ruffled even her father, who understood best those who fit the mold of their culture. Van, an unruly child, might better have belonged to Foster, once styled Bananas.

As we watch the eggs boil in my kitchen, Van asks, "What do you want to be called?"

"Do I have to be called something?"

"Dad said to ask you."

"He would."

Grudgingly she smiles. She is terribly thin in a string-tied halter that shows protruding shoulder bones. She occupies the seat that is sometimes Roy's, sitting with her elbows on the shelf-table much as he sits. Instead of a beer she has carrot juice because she is into health however much her flesh resists it. Her waist-length hair is straight as a string and somewhat the same color.

The difference is that when Roy is here he tells all that is bothering him by the way he moves and his tone of voice. And when it is off his chest he can get back to the business of getting along or screwing up or whatever. Van, however, seems to be peering at me from the deep recesses of a chamber with bars on the window. Her face is without expression and her feelings are locked inside. Yet this is not unpleasant; it is like looking at a pond with no ripples on the surface.

"You can call me Foster."

"You don't want Mrs. Landrum or something?"

"Foster is something."

"Where'd you get a name like that?"

"I inherited it from my daddy; the other name, Beverly, I try to forget."

"I know about that, changing your name. I call myself Vanessa at school, if you can believe that. Van isn't short for anything; it's just short."

"Do you like it better being Vanessa?"

"It doesn't really solve anything."

"True. For years I signed my name Bananas Foster on my homework, but it didn't help my grades."

She smiles that hesitant smile. "You should have kept that name; it's a dessert you know."

There is a passivity about her which is very appealing, as if she were going to do nothing to keep the hurricane from blowing her down or the train from running into her. There's the impression that she is sitting composed with folded hands in the eyes of the storm, waiting for it to happen to her.

"Van, do you mind that Ben may move in here?"

She shrugs an elaborate, lengthy shrug that sharpens her collar bone and shoulder blades. "Why should I?"

"Because of your mother."

"I'm not even going out there to see her."

"How can you decide that?"

"She wouldn't know I came."

"Ben says that, that she doesn't know him, but I have this feeling that she is inside of herself screaming at you through her eyes. I think about her, about how it would be to be there. You might look so different to other people if you were in, and your mouth and hands might act like someone else was pulling the strings. But you would know if your daughter said your name." This is thinking aloud and not solely aimed at my still companion. "Ben isn't going back; you must."

"He never understood my mother at all. He thought she was something and she was something else. He thinks I'm this hippie, this estranged generation-gap stuff, this other person. If you want to live with somebody like him, it's nothing to me. He's mad I didn't answer his letters about you, but there's no making sense out of his letters. I never bother to answer them any more."

"He's afraid maybe that you are going to judge him for what happened to your mother."

"No, he's not. He doesn't like to see me because I remind him of all that's over. He'd rather pretend that none of the time when she lost the baby and then got bad ever had to do with him. Some people learn from their mistakes and some people look at them like they were watching this rerun movie on TV that's all about someone else."

"It reassures him that he is starting over with me."

"And with Hannah. She's his kind of daughter. He thinks she's just great because she's not nuts like the rest of us. He wrote me a whole letter about her engagement party, if you can believe it."

"What did he say?" What would he want to tell Van about that stiff evening of champagne and flowers?

"Some of the usual stuff about ceremonies. Forgive me if I forget entirely but all his letters sound alike."

"Hannah has been to see him on the campus."

"I can see her knocking on his door, giving her impression that every day is a big birthday party." She looks at me with an unhappy face. "And when I go over there and knock on his door he'll say, 'What are *you* doing here?'"

"You and Hannah are dreadful together."

"I know it." She sinks her face into her thin hands. "I hate her actually. Or used to, way back. She still looks at me like I was a freak or a cripple."

The eggs boil over on the stove and make water and foam on the burner. We set them to cool, and, in another bowl, mix sweet pickle relish and apple and green pepper. I shuck yellow corn and slice onions and zucchini to go with the salad. Van is pleased with all the vegetables and helps with the corn. Her presence makes me feel like a truck farmer working on my home-grown produce. Earlier she fixed us a large bowl of nut and fruit granola, laden with vitamins and calories, for tomorrow's breakfast (which will put another distance between my daughter and my daughter-to-be). For supper she wants to make us cornbread from the recipe on the cornmeal sack.

It is strange how her alienation, her inwardness, turns the unlikely pair of us into domestics. In some way that does not get explored, we are breaking bread together.

"I have imagined your mother, Vanessa, until I think I know her."

"She's not really crazy."

"What is she really?"

She chews on a halter string. "Like the rest of us:

mixed up. Not sure what's real and what isn't. The only reason she's in there and we're not is that she couldn't handle it; she had to leave, any way she could."

"Ben must look for women like that."

"If it wouldn't hurt your feelings, I was going to say that. You're like she was, part of you is somewhere else. But lots of us are that way and we don't get put away. The difference is its not too much for you, like it was for her. She thought if she looked pretty and smiled a lot that would make it all come out right."

"Ben said you were getting your degree in psychology."

"He has to have a name for everything so he can file it and forget it. He thinks if he says to himself often enough that's what I'm doing and he's paying for it, then he has done his bit. He never asks me about my work with the autistic kids because he doesn't want to hear about it. He doesn't like to hear about unpleasant things, which fits right in, because she didn't like to admit that there were unpleasant things. They were a pair."

"You plan to work with children like that?"

She stirs the meal and eggs awhile. "This guy I'm shacking up with says we ought to take off and live a year in Mexico first."

"Do you want to?"

"I guess I don't care. I've got the rest of my life to test crazy kids." She tells me about this life's work, in her offhand way making it clear that she has no other choice. "I'm only going to work with the real little kids, the ones you can spot early and do something about. You know," she demonstrates with a strand of her own tan hair, "some of them eat their hair and some of them eat string. They're really messed up." But this is shrugged off, too. "But before that, being with him and going down to Yucatan is okay. Anyway, you can't test crazies without a master's."

How fearless of this thin girl to intend to go back in and hold hands with all her past influences. How casually she offers to carry the load for all her family. Most of us do not do that; most of us dump the past wholly on our family's insufficient laps.

When supper is all ready and put aside, we sit together in a silence that is like being alone, when one does not smile or gesture or appear busy. Van's eyes at first are closed as if she were meditating and her body is limp and still. Then after a time she opens them, looks at me and waits. As if it were my turn to talk.

Because she is the sort of person who looks so direct and expects you to level, there is no alternative but to do so. Her listening face reminds me of one of Borges' tales when he has created a distinct universe and invites you in. Soon I am talking about how it was for me with my parents and how it was living in that house of Mother's and then how it was being a mother myself and how you find that you are doing some of the very same things they did or you are knocking your head against the wall, like Mildred, to do just the opposite, and it still comes out more or less the same. Like Mother, Mildred gets her picture in the local gazette. How Hannah is more like my sisters than my sisters.

It is to some extent what Henry and I have talked about, families, but Van understands the part of it below the surface, that you never get loose from your family and that you are your family but that you have to find a way to transmute your past so you can be the beginning of you. I don't do well saying it but she does so well hearing it that the slightest stammer communicates.

When all that is laid out and we have accepted it and she has thought about chewing her tan hair, she makes a personal offering to me in return.

"Dad didn't tell you, did he, that I write poetry." This is not a question.

"No. Does he know it?"

"I've sent him some." She considers it. "My teachers say it's too moody. But that is what poetry is about, moods." She tucks her legs up crosslegged like a yogi. "It's good. My stuff. But I don't show it very much."

"I would like to see it."

"Dad blots it out because Mother wrote poems, too. They rhymed and they had all the proper feet per line; strictly they made sense, but it was like each one had a big empty hole in the middle."

"I used to make up places I had never been to, to imagine I was from. It was a way to get out of Sally, Texas. There was a farm by a pond that was shaded by cypress trees. It had rolling green hills and lots of Poland-China pigs."

"Poetry isn't an escape like that. Not for me."

"What is it?"

She twists her hair and closes her eyes. "I don't know. Joe, that's this boy, says if you talk about it it dissipates it." She looks uncertain. "You can see. It's more moods, I guess."

Supper goes as expected. Hannah tries earnestly to make us into one happy family, an almost-legal mother and father and two daughters who have known each other since they started fifth grade. She introduces bits of conversation and eats with her very best manners. Her tone is of a girl chatting with Uncle Dick's mother or Eugene's mother or the pastor at her aunt's church. She pats her mouth with her napkin often and neatly.

Van eats with her face closed and blank. She is very Zen about her meal: she sees her food, she chews her food, she swallows her food. She takes no notice of Hannah and when she breathes in air, between bites, she makes dry empty sounds.

Hannah mentions Eugene's name and their plans for the evening. This gives her comfort as it makes clear she is almost part of his family; also, Eugene is not interested in Van. Last night when he met Van he reacted like a gentleman. There she stood in her T shirt, without a bra, and Eugene, in his straight and honest way, had not averted his level brown eyes. But when she was gone he assured Hannah, "She's not even pretty, is she?"

Hannah tells about Jenny Sue's Easter plans and how awful it is that spring vacation and Easter aren't the same week this year at the university and how lucky Van is that she gets such a long time off, and how this messes up Jenny Sue's family, who always goes to the coast for Easter.

She likes stories of families whose annual events never vary, who always vacation at their cabin, who always observe Christmas with their grandparents. These are signs of constancy missing from her own life which even Dorothy and Mildred cannot make up for. Jenny Sue's family also has a poodle who always plays in the surf at the shore.

Van does not react to a poodle at the beach. Overwhelmed by this tale she has gone into herself in a withdrawn and fragile way that must have echoes of her mother.

This does not appeal to Ben. He keeps glancing at his daughter and muttering about the food which seems to him on a par with the faculty dining room; he cannot understand why we are eating egg salad for a dinner meal but he understands quite clearly that this is his child's fault.

"Ben, you must give me the names of whomever you want to invite to my wedding." Hannah makes a point to use this first name here, in front of his daughter, to show how well she knows him. "You and Mother both, before Eugene's mother fills up all the seats in that small church." She is proud of all the friends Eugene's family has. Besides, the wedding seems the only sure topic. It is not her fault if the other daughter is not having one, and there are lots of details like this that we all need to work on together.

Ben makes some lengthy talk about his various colleagues and the department head, eliminating some and leaving others. He avoids his daughter's eyes in this charade which he puts on to create an aura of fatherhood in his life.

"Mother? Don't you want at least to invite Mr. Moore and your friend Clarice Watson and your old friend that we lived with when I was a little girl?"

My guests at the wedding are all my family and some past and future husbands. What more can she expect of me? Answer: an old school chum in a peach silk dress who dabs at her eyes with a monogrammed handkerchief. This is all out of proportion. Van manages these alliances of the body without such fanfare. Why don't we? "Henry and Shirley are all, honey, besides the family. Clarice is a woman from the welfare department that I've only laid eyes on three times, and Meg and I have lost touch. Besides, she's still in Seattle last I heard."

Hannah lays down her fork. Her voice quivers, "But, Mother, you *told* me—" She has heard the truth, offhand.

Van rouses herself. "Why did you lose touch with her?"

"She got married."

Van nods as if that made it all clear. "I guess that's bound to happen. Now that I'm living with Joe I never even see my old roommate."

Hannah does not understand. "But Jenny Sue and I have even more to talk about now that I'm engaged than we did when we were pledges."

Van cuts off this Jenny Sue. "I would never talk about Joe to anyone else, that's why."

Hannah flushes, put down by both of us. "I don't believe I have ever met Mr. Moore's wife, have I?" She is very formal and distant with me. Implies that he may not have one.

Ben says, "You haven't missed much." Trying to help out this talk he expands on Shirley at her worst at the open house.

"I was at the Sweetheart dance," Hannah tells him, "I couldn't come."

There is the sound of plates being cleared and everyone stacking and folding, ill at ease, waiting for dessert.

Ben tries to get us back to the ceremony, to safe ground. "At least now that I've signed all the papers and paid off the lawyer you've got plenty of people to give you away."

"You are divorced." His daughter states flatly a fact she has heard for the first time in public.

"As of yesterday." He does not look at her.

"Ben, you don't mind, do you, really, that Daddy is

coming? I mean, since he wanted to do this and he *is* my father. And if you and mother are married by then you will be in the receiving line anyway."

The only benefit of our being married before Hannah is that when the CPA came I could tell him that none of us need his name any more, that he can take his Landrum and cram it, that we are each vesting ourselves in new ones, belonging to men named Roberts and Bracken, and would he like back rent for the years we have borrowed his?

Ben makes light of his replacement. "Don't worry; I'll be the usher who walks your mother down the aisle."

"That would be perfect, Ben, because then you could just sit down with her. And Daddy is going to sit by Eugene's mother after he tells the preacher he is giving me away. That way nothing will be awkward or anything, and he's going to be staying with them anyway and . . ."

The Sally *Sentinel* could do this so much better. I interrupt her orderly procession of niceties. "We must be sure to get a photograph of the father of the bride beside the mother of the groom. His boutonniere was in a shade to match her imported voile garden dress."

Van takes in the appearance of this second absent parent. She looks at us and there is a darkness in her eyes. "And maybe Mom will come," she says, "and she can sit in the back row with me." She finishes our meal with a shrill, splintering laugh.

Van goes with me this morning to HEXPOP. It is a place to go to get up her nerve to visit her father at his office. She chews on a fingernail as I open the mail and get coffee. At first she is still half here and half there, somewhere else.

"Dad never told me what you did," she says, reading a

Halt Exponential Population Growth flyer. "I thought you were a teacher or something. I guess because everybody is a teacher."

"Was your mother?"

"For a year. Till she got pregnant with me. So that doesn't count because I only heard about it. She talked about it like she had done it for forty years. It made an impression on her, but it was only one year actually."

While she looks around I skim the stacks of population bulletins and reports on my desk. Some items are saved to headline the next issue of the newsletter; some are circled and put in a folder for possible brochures. There are new and drastic proposals to limit birth: a public health plan from the People's Republic of China calling for sexual abstinence among young people during the years when fertility and desire are high; a British scientist with a scheme to produce a preponderance of male children to insure an immediate decline in the birth rate. But these will not be given much notice. Research has got to get at the basic fact of how to provide a way not to conceive. And I have got to get at a way to tell about all of this that will speak to women. Both those here, and far from here.

Van turns her attention fully to the stack of papers. She concentrates now, in her total way, making the effort to see and understand what holds me here. It is touching to watch her frown and follow the words with her eyes, as she does not see it in the same context as I do at all.

"India is fifty million condoms short in 1973," she reads aloud, wrapping a string of hair around her finger. "It sounds like they mean short condoms. Anyway, how could you tell how many they need? How do you decide how many each man gets? A condom per man or one per screw?" She picks up another story, "Look at this: a report on sperm maturation in the epididymis of rabbits and bulls. Don't people laugh at you about all this?"

"We take it all seriously. Because it is." She should see that.

She asks, "What are you working on now?"

I talk to her about the abortion decision, and about an idea to show that any form of birth control, even terminating pregnancies, is preferable to such alternatives as the battered child. Glad to have a sounding board I hand her a sketch of an eighteenth-century English countryside, with a quote about its overcrowding, lack of sanitation and heavy crop failure. The illustration is of a documented form of infanticide: a mother pushing her unwanted infant beneath the wheels of a tumbril. Something then needs to be said on the facing page for abortion. But I am uncertain: it may be like the dog pound.

Van studies it a long time and hands it back. "I don't think it is as simple as that. Lots of times the very parents who want kids most damage them the worst. I've seen this with the crazies I work with: they were planned for, they weren't birth control failures most of them, but the mothers go berserk, they have all this hate inside or some of them just have a vacuum."

"I guess I am talking about the unwanted ones." She has been closer to reality than I have.

"I know. Nothing is all one thing or the other. But like we all use something, the pill, the IUD, some girls get those shots, nobody trusts rubbers, we're thinking about ourselves and how we aren't ready to start all that baby thing yet. And maybe some of us won't ever, the mess we've seen it lead to, the way people screw kids up. But about battered kids nobody I know would do that even if she did get pregnant. So I don't see that what you're saying is the point. What I'm saying is that being a decent human being to your child has nothing to do with birth control it seems to me."

Henry comes from behind the wall to see who is in his reception area. "This your daughter?" he asks me, giving Van a hug on general principles.

She shrinks from him as I tell him she is Ben's and visiting. Can it have been that long since he has seen Hannah? Is that because she does not come here as she is embarrassed to be connected with my office; or do I not invite her because it is such a relief for me to have this square footage where my name is not *Oh, Mother*.

Henry bustles about to show our visitor who is in charge. He mentions charts, graphs, quotes, and statistics that he expects from me by tomorrow for the newsletter. He is sweating hard, his tie is off, he is working on his vital contribution, the editorial. "Glad you're here," he says to Van. "See that she doesn't goof off. I'm kidding, she's one of your better workers."

When he is out of sight Van sits in my client's chair with her legs straight before her. She is digesting a new thought and after a silence says, "Tell me about him." Pointing toward Henry's office.

"He has a wife who can't cook and one time he lived on nothing but grits and he can sell anything to anybody." She understands that the real Henry in his carefully buttoned thirty-six-average suit is his private business.

Squinting her eyes at some far-off place, Van asks, "What I mean is, what is it like working with a man all day?"

"You forget that after a while."

"Like when you're in class with guys you don't care about."

"Somewhat."

"I could do that. I used to worry about when I got a job. It seems like I have to get involved with anybody I'm around a lot. That's strange, too, because in high school I didn't even talk to boys."

"It must depend on the man. Like there are some women you could work with twenty years and never get close to." Like Clarice.

Henry sticks his head back around. He has put on his tie and slicked down his hair. "May I take you girls out to lunch in a spell? My treat."

"Thank you, Henry. We're meeting Ben."

He smites his forehead. "Should have figured that. Bet he's glad to have you here in town, young lady."

"Don't bet too much." Unexpectedly, Van smiles at him.

Henry laughs over that and shakes his head; after all he was just being polite, if anybody knows about families he does.

Van paces around the room, stares out the window at the day, comes back to where I sit. "Should I go on over to his office?"

"You'll have more to say to him there than you did at our supper table. He won't be acting like a father."

"He'll have students there." She chews on a strand of hair.

"You're a student."

Her kinship with her father, which is not pleasing to either of them, is still strong enough to bring her here for spring break and strong enough to bring Ben to the verge of guilt in his dealings with her. Van and Ben cannot be strangers to one another; like all of us, they cannot escape relationship.

"I'll meet you there," I tell her, needing to work awhile.

"Doesn't he ever come get you here?"

"His office is nearer the food."

"I guess I'll go." She edges toward the door, her eyes now withdrawn, her hands searching for pockets to hide in. "You will come?"

"At noon."

"He'll have to stay and talk to me if he knows you're going to come."

But Van is gone when I get there. Ben claims she turned on her heel and walked out without a word, that he has no idea what got into her, that he has never understood her. He says he hadn't said two words to her before she started to cry in that spooky way she has when no sound comes out and she doesn't move her face but she is crying anyway. And then she did what infuriates him the most: she began to chew on her hair. "She is as out of it as her mother." He is slumped down in his professor's chair.

"She sees things clearer than anyone I know."

"Then what does that make me?"

"Her father."

"As Borges would say: the world unfortunately is real; I, unfortunately, am me."

He gets up and goes through the leave-taking process of removing pencils from his pocket, closing folders, checking his calendar, looking vaguely about his office to imprint its disorder on his mind, to fasten it into place until he returns.

As we head for the stairs, I say, "Let's don't get married, Ben." Looking at him through the finely cut prism of his daughter's perspective, I see a man who contributes with all good intentions to our all becoming less than we are, less glued together, less clear. Somehow his view of us as archetypes must unhinge us as particular women. Why else does he collect the two Vans and Foster. Why else did even the girl by the Coke machine flee in distraction to Barnard?

"What are you talking about? After all that divorce cost me?" Ben takes my arm and pilots me out onto the sidewalk in the direction of the faculty dining room. He handles me in the reflex way you deal with those who need guidance.

"I want to eat up the street where the students eat. Hamburgers."

"We haven't got time to walk all that way."

"We can make time."

"It's always mobbed; there's no room to breathe and you can't hear yourself think."

"It can be mobbed for once with me."

Why can't I eat hamburgers at lunch? Students do. They don't sit at a homemade counter watching the yard turn brown in the sun; they don't eat the faculty's salmon loaf and pudding. They eat shakes and fries; and none of them gets married.

"Ben, after while we may not even like each other. And there will be all those *meals*."

With Hannah gone I could live for a time in that stucco house and call it Foster's place. I could live a private separate life. Why can't Ben be content to bring me wine

and share my bed? Why must professors take wives . . .
"My head hurts."

"You never have headaches."

"I'm learning."

"What happened?" He takes my hand and frowns as if trying to relate to this irregular behavior. As if trying to figure out what a hike up the drag has got to do with it.

I say, "Van left." And I am scared.

"She makes a habit of that." He writes off her behavior.

We do find the hamburger place and Ben delights in it. He has no complaints about the food; he has refilled his own coffee cup, enjoying elbowing, literally, his way through the throng of students. He is an ordinary-looking man enacting the part of professor, waving to everyone he recognizes, calling out the names he remembers. His hair curling down the back of his neck into his collar, and his large nose sunburned from hiking across the campus, he now busies himself with finishing a very hot fried apple pie dusted with cinnamon and sugar.

I press my wrists against the cool sides of the paper cup of iced tea and say, "Lots of people don't get married."

But Ben cannot imagine not partaking of the culture's favorite institution. Defensively he tells me, "Lots of people don't go through all the hassle of getting unmarried either."

"Hannah said she ate two orders of french fries here." So many girls like her are here with hair and pink cheeks, clustered together; so many others, too, who look like Van, distant, jeaned, with a rain of flat hair, sit alone.

"It's good to have one daughter who's easy to please."

I can imagine Hannah here with Ben, her father-to-be, showing him off to the song leader and the chaplain and a table full of pledges, letting herself be persuaded to lengthen lunch by eating french fry after french fry dipped bite by bite in catsup, making eager talk to the one supportive adult besides her aunts that her mother has given her.

How can I deny Ben to my daughter just because my head hurts and my feet are cold, or, rather, because he brought his daughter today to anguish and silence, not for the first time and not for the last.

"Hannah wants you to be her father." That seems relevant at this time.

"So don't balk at the last minute." He wipes sugar from his mouth.

It is not pleasant to think that you get married for other people. Surely young Kermit, red-faced and fresh off the farm, did not realize as he fumbled with Opal's cotton blouse, that what was happening was due in part to Opal's father having left one rained-out day for better soil. It is hard to accept that you are never without those others.

It is clear to me that when you marry there will be voices in your ear from which you are never free. There will be comment every time you let some acquaintance in the back door for a late-night snack or stay too long over a pitcher of dark beer at a pleasant cafe, or walk downtown along the river and forget to come on home until long past dark, or even elect not to fix that ever-present evening meal. There will be my mother saying, "Beverly, you never give a thought to what people will think." There will be Hannah, asking, "Mother, where were you?"

"I got cold feet, Ben."

"That's better. The long walk was worth it to warm them up." He reaches for my hand to knead it. "I won't be bad to have around," he says, wanting me to want the job. He rubs my knee with his under the table.

"We could both do worse." I admit this much.

"Come on, we're better at it than that. You're running down my hidden talents."

"I have no complaints on that score." Either I am or I'm not going to marry him, and if I am, there is no need to force the difficulty of the decision on Ben. I put my hand on his knee and he feels things are fine again and finishes off the last of my fried pie.

It is a public place and therefore a fitting place to agree to commit an act I have not committed in twenty years: marriage. This, then, is my final act of charity for Hannah-spelled-backward, to promise to abide this man until his bushy hair is white and his open face as lined as an old man's hand. It will be worth some compromise to hear her say, when Ben and I stand joined in holy matrimony, me in a drab blue dress selected especially for the occasion: "Oh, Mother, you really do look *nice*."

We eat, because Hannah is here, at the dining table. Because she is here I wait the table, bringing in our tomato soup and cheese sandwiches and our iced tea and her cookies and my coffee, all in proper containers. We eat with proper silverware and use cloth napkins that will have to be washed and ironed again.

In the kitchen my shelf is folded under the window to make a larger passageway. Vanessa has been gone a week.

This table set for lunch for two seems far too crowded with spoons, forks, bowls, cups, mats, napkins, lemon slices, and our expectations for one another. It was not worth such effort just for the taste of toaster-browned white bread and metallic canned soup. With Roy or Van a meal was limited to the act of eating itself—that plus a space of time to talk, empty time that felt as easy as taking off your shoes.

"I miss Van," I admit.

"She wrote to you, didn't she?" Hannah asks in a non-committal voice. She stares at her sandwich plate, which has been garnished with a pickle and a handful of potato chips.

"A very Zen letter. The boy she is shacking up with is in a depression. The crazies she is watching the prof test are very playful. Ohio is green and wet." The words are mine but the flat linear delineation of vital matters is hers. She writes of her life very much as if she were saying: my enemies are ill; my friends now grow orchids.

Hannah wipes her neat mouth slowly with her linen napkin. "You don't even mind, do you?"

"What?" I like the style; it seems Chinese and real.

"You don't even mind that Van, Jr., is openly sleeping with a person who is doing badly in school and doesn't want to do anything at all but paint his pictures. She told me so herself."

"That isn't my affair; I do care if she is doing all right."

"I mean, you have one set of values for me and I have always tried to do everything you wanted me to, just the way you wanted me to, and then you have another set for her." Hannah holds her napkin tightly in her white hand. Her face is white and very still in the center of its wreath of hair. As I watch, she starts to cry. "You always liked her best. Always."

"She wasn't mine to raise. I don't have to worry over

what she does. I think she does so well considering the bad time with her mother." How is there any way to explain?

Hannah pushes back her chair but does not rise. "All the time she was here you two were in the kitchen making things like cornbread. You never do that with me. You say you hate to cook but all the time she was here you fixed fresh green beans and corn on the cob." Her voice cracks. "You even made Aunt Gladys' potato pancakes which you never made in my whole life."

"But that was what she wanted to do. With you I do what you like to do—" Why else are we two using all this silver and drinking soup from tureens with handles on a busy weekday evening when I had rather be through and out of here, my one plate in the sink?

"You took her to your office, didn't you, and went to lunch with her and Ben. You never went with me and Ben. You never asked me to come see you at your office. In the whole year and a half that I have been on campus you never one time, not even on Founders' Day, came and had lunch with me at the house. There are some mothers who don't even live in the same town who come in once a month to eat lunch at the house with their daughters. One of them, even, who is a senior, her mother has done that since she was a freshman."

"Did you ask me to?"

"You knew they served to guests. You remember that Mrs. Archer said at the tea that you must come eat with the girls sometime. We talked about the guest charge on the bill." She is weeping quietly on her dress front.

Slowly she gets up and folds her napkin neatly beside her plate. Mannerly even now, she pats her damp hair, and with a small hand wipes her tear-streaked face. With dignity she carries her plate to the kitchen and sets it on the drain. When I follow her in she turns her face to me, and it exposes all her misery. "You'd rather have that girl here who is right out in the open all the things you didn't want me to be. She's even tried *pot*."

Yes, of course. Van's even tried disorder and mistakes and failure and more than one boy. And if Hannah has not, who but me is to take the blame?

"Don't cry, honey. Please."

"My whole life since I can remember I have tried to do everything just the way you wanted me to and take advice from Aunt Mildred and Aunt Dorothy and not do anything that would make you mad or make you ashamed of me or anything. And do everything all right in school so you would be proud when you talked to my teachers. And even make sure that nobody was ever allowed to criticize you, because you were my mother." She rubs a fist on a streaked cheek and stares at me as if she had finally to look at what was there, "And nothing I ever did, not ever, was what you wanted, Mother."

There is so little to say in defense of what is true. Lamely I try to offer up something that will heal this somewhat. "I didn't know about the lunch," I tell her, coming to where she stands. "I have a new friend named Alice Jean and we were going to eat at someplace where neither of us poured the coffee. Maybe you would like to come along and meet her?" Your mother's friend.

Hannah claps her hands over her ears and turns her face to the wall. "Don't tell me any more about your made-up friends. Have the decency at least not to lie to me any more, Mother."

"She was at the open house."

"All that time you fed me those stories about Clarice Watson, making a fool of me, when you hardly knew her to speak to. You admitted that to Van." She turns back to me and takes her hands down. "You never, ever, told me the truth about anybody, not your mother and daddy, or Aunt Dorothy and Uncle Charlie, or probably not even D-Daddy." Years of unsaid words overwhelm her. Her mouth quivers; her eyes blink back fresh tears. She has the face of a child, betrayed. In a final thrust that comes out of her very depths, she whispers, "I guess you even s-slept with Roy. I guess that night we caught you wasn't the only night he came." She stares at me to let the enormity of her words sink into both of us. She speaks in anger against all those who are close to her mother. With a final look she slams the door between us to the hall.

I hear her go past the crowded pantry and up the stairs.

The dishes stand in the sink. Out the window the green spring grass receives twilight, and the air smells of crab apple. Nineteen years ago there was running water in the old stone fountain. For nineteen years I have worked to make a girl who for nineteen years has worked to please her mother.

I bury my head in my shirtwaist arms on the counter and weep for all of us everywhere who breed ourselves into families, for all of us everywhere who are never enough for one another.

Hannah comes down in a pink blouse and short skirt to wait for Eugene. She is washed and has a fresh face on and gives me a daughter's kiss when she finds me in a straight chair, looking at the back yard.

"I'm really sorry, Mother. I guess I got the jitters. With the wedding so close and all."

"Roy only ate peanut butter here."

But the time between us is closed as a river after a stone has sunk from sight. It is as if we were back in the past with Roger and me fighting and accusing: Hannah has left the room to put herself in her bed and sing and pat her doll. "Honest, Mother, you know I didn't mean all that."

She is composed and bland. She touches her emerald-cut diamond for comfort, and says, "If it's all right with you, Jenny Sue and I are going to spend the night on campus. The housemother said we could because so many people are gone for the weekend. And Eugene promised to have me in by twelve."

11. The Wedding

We drive to Dorothy's for Hannah's wedding day. Dorothy does not live far from us, past a few quicklime plants, and across a minor river, but hers seems another, more southern world as her life is contained in this small shady town and because her yard looks year round like a home on a garden tour pilgrimage. She lives in the part of central Texas where each small town has a fine courthouse in a square, and each small town has one or two medallion homes over a hundred years old, which is a pioneer house to us. She lives where towns are not far from fences and pastures of thick grasses for dairy cows.

Dorothy and I hug and whisper in her kitchen. She has slipped out of her shoes, as her feet are swollen from the day's work. Her kitchen is a green, inhabited place; we stand beneath climbing vines and hanging baskets. Through the window you can see masses of brilliant potted flowers on the patio and along the low brick wall beside the curved pool. She wears a billowing shift that falls to her ankles in a soft print with leaves and blooms like those about us which grow from her caresses and April's sun. It is as if the plants she tends had covered her with their own protecting foliage. She is at home in her house.

"If she calls me 'sister' one more time, I'll scream," she says, wilting under too much management.

The wedding, because Mother is here, has made each of us behave like ourselves, only more so. Mildred has pressed her fingers to her temples in an effort to organize this long unstructured afternoon. Dorothy has, in turn, grown slower, heavier and kinder to everyone. Beverly has felt out of place.

Mother is fulsome with the chance to be a bride again and spent the cold buffet lunch telling, down to the smallest details, endlessly repeating herself in her joy, of Mildred's wedding, of Dorothy's, of Aunt Gladys', of hers, such a showpiece the county had never seen, and even of mine, belatedly, as this child for whom we gather is mine. "The Foster girls," she says, to anyone who will listen, "were lovely brides." Under her watchful eye we become daughters again. Mildred manages, Dorothy charms, Beverly longs to escape.

The men have retired to Charlie's cork-floored room

with a bar. Daddy is like a boy playing hooky. He is his most sociable self among his kin, and with his afternoon beer he sits as if at the old kitchen table or the counter of the old drugstore telling anecdotes to all his secondhand sons.

Dick has talked to Ben, the newcomer, about the mounting urgency of the energy crisis which no one is going to take seriously until it is too late. "In Colorado," he said, "right now there are service stations running out of gas and tourists returning home. By next winter . . ." Charlie has told them all that these church weddings are just like they were in his day, but, like everything else, they get harder and more expensive the second time around. Daddy has taken to Ben, a new face, and the two of them traded all the old farm stories including the one about the bull who leaped the fence.

In addition to this, Mildred has been by the country club three times already to be sure the reception will unveil her finest efforts in taste and color scheme. With Mother following.

It is no wonder this is getting to Dorothy.

"Don't mind her," I tell my younger sister, "Mother is driving her crazy."

"She wants us all back again just like we were. Poor Mother."

"Poor us."

"Still, it's harder on the children. Mildred's and mine make each other fuss or else the big ones tease. It's hard for them to play all day together."

"I think Mildred instructs hers to pinch yours."

She giggles. "You know when Charlie and I lived in that apartment on Rio Grande street that we had to walk up a flight of stairs to get to, and he was studying all the time, and then I thought I was pregnant, we used to make each other these promises about what we would never do with our children. We were both the babies of our families you know and that makes you really have older parents, his particularly."

"You weren't pregnant then."

"It was sure a relief. Charlie would really have been mad at me." She wipes her warm face. "It worked out all right. But when ours did come along so fast we forgot all that and now we baby the baby like we said we never would. But him being a boy, too."

"You're good with all of them."

"Charlie is so careful not to push them into anything like he was pushed. We may be too easygoing, not just on them but on ourselves, too." She pats her plump arms self-consciously. "I guess that's what we have in common." She looks up at me fondly. "I can't imagine being with anyone but Charlie. Don't you think things tend to work out? Like you and Ben."

Yes, if work out means the way we deal with life. People like her accept; people like me survive. And I would never trade. "I really do, Dot. I really do." We press cheeks and I suggest, "Let's get some tea and sit outside."

"Where's Hannah?"

"She's lying down upstairs."

Dorothy has arranged for Hannah and her friends to have the guest room and bath to use for hanging their dresses before the ceremony, putting on their faces, helping one another get ready and looking after treasures like the bride's blue garter, and the string of pearls from Eugene. Dorothy has turned down the sheets for naps and filled the dressing table with spring bouquets. She has done all the small kindnesses such as keeping a shelf in her refrigerator for cold Dr. Peppers.

"Let's go up there," she says, "in that bedroom with the window fan and the shades down. Doesn't that sound like the best idea you ever heard? I wouldn't mind getting off my feet, either."

"You go up with her. She would really like to be with you. I think she's nervous." After all these endless months of planning each detail until it is rehearsed and set in cement, Hannah has turned limp and white today. Nineteen is too young to give yourself away.

I take my tea out to a corner of the garden filled only with hedges and bedded plants. Charlie sits there with a glass of bourbon.

"Sorry." I have intruded.

"Stick around. I had enough of your old man and his stockyard jokes."

"He is so happy to be here."

"They must not let him out on a pass very often."

"Something like that."

Charlie is my ally after last night when he rescued me at the rehearsal dinner from Roger, an old husband of mine, who spent the evening on the mauve arm of Eugene's mother when he was not leading his daughter in practice runs down the aisle.

The only consolation in seeing Roger after such a long time was that he was nothing to wish I had seen sooner. We had got together once through some accident of time and place and it shouldn't happen twice. He apparently thought the same of me in my perennial aqua dress.

Because there was no one else around to do it, I had

227

to introduce him to Charlie. Not a scene I had imagined for myself. But Charlie said smoothly, "Oh, you're the one who stole my girl."

To which Roger, not to be outdone, had tipped his handsome head and replied, "We both lost a good thing, Charlie."

"Hannah was delighted you could come," I told Roger, civilized.

"Wouldn't miss it for the world," he said, the same.

Later, after we had finished dinner and wine, and all the toasts had been made, and blushes blushed, he sidled up again to try to get in a few words. He still played the part of spectator with his camera in his pocket and his way of repeating everyone's name over when he was introduced. "Beverly, as long as I am here I thought perhaps we might have a few words. Our daughter is certainly . . ."

And out of nowhere was Charlie's jowly face. "I already have this dance. See, here's my name on her dance card." And holding up an imaginary program, he whisked me out the double doors onto the country club patio and presented me to Ben. "Quit competing for father-of-the-bride and look after the one you came with, will you?"

Now in this still green spot I tell him honestly from my heart, "Charlie, you can call me any time you're in town. You really were a lifesaver with the crumb last night."

"You got your back up when I said that Thanksgiving" —he looks at me with his puffy eyes—"but I thought we could have a cup of coffee once in a while. Hell, that's all water over the dam."

"I know that. Old water. Old, old dam."

"All I can remember of that time if you want the truth is my dad pressuring me to get to med school, telling me to watch out about the girls or I'd never get to med school. Every time I got a girl in the car alone I'd hear him saying, 'You better watch out, son,' and then, there I was, finally out of med school, with a family started already, and hell, it's hard to see what it's been for. One of these days I'm going to look up and say, 'Charlie, old buddy, your life is all water over the dam.'"

"I think about that with Hannah getting married. Was this what I spent all those years growing her up for?"

"Yeah, it'll be Dottie one of these days. It isn't what it's cracked up to be." He lids his eyes and drains his glass. "So why're you doing it again?"

"You make decisions."

"Or they make you, right?" He gives me an echo of the old grin. "Agreed?"

Ben locates us to say that it is time to get some pictures made and then head toward the church. He looks tired of Daddy too.

"It's not Roger and his tripod?"

"He'll catch you at the church."

"Charlie, thanks for last night."

"Any time." He gets up.

"And thanks for the part of this bill you're footing."

"Just getting in practice, with three of my own coming along." He eyes Ben as if trying to see the point.

Ben grabs my hand and leads me to the house. "This place," he says, disgruntled, tired of my kin, "is haunted by your exes."

"You're just mad because Roger is outfathering you."

Mother, omnipresent, is delighted to catch Beverly holding hands with her gentleman friend.

It seems quite final getting into my mother-of-the-bride dress, a new drab blue gown that looks like water-marked moiré, with a row of buttons down the front that my fingers find clumsy. It is a garment so especially chosen and so appropriate that there seems to be no turning back.

The dress was the last decision my daughter and I made together. Our next to last was that, for the duration of the wedding, the bride, the mother of the bride, and the father of the bride would all have the same last name. To hurry up a marriage to Ben seemed like a shotgun wedding. So, despite their arguments, it was agreed to put it off until hot weather, until school was out. But to set her mind at rest Ben and I have set a definite date: later.

All week has been as charged as the moment before the organist plays the first bars of the wedding march. Hannah set up her presents on the table in the dining room and opened the house for viewing, as is the custom. The old crowd of girls came by and had punch and admired her things: the mixing bowls, Teflon pans, china in her selected pattern, the myriad containers and appliances for cooking and serving. It may have been the sight of that gift-laden table covered in an organdy cloth that moved my own marriage until summer when tomatoes and cantaloupe abound and tuna fish is acceptable for supper.

Even Roy came by with a present. "Guess you'll be glad when this shit is over?"

"I can make it through Saturday."

"You having a bunch of family here?"

"At Dorothy's. The sister with the flowers has the church."

"That figures. A virgin white bride has to have a big,

showy church, the kind where you got to rent a tux and do the whole show."

He produced a Lone Star beer for each of us, a treat, to drink from the cold cans while we walked around the dining table and sized up the treasures. Hannah had made a white centerpiece with plastic baby's-breath and satin ribbons, and put white tapers in new silver candlesticks from Jenny Sue's family. We walked round and round the table with neither of us talking. What was there to say that needed to be said?

"She out with him selecting the john paper?"

"She's at the bridesmaids' luncheon."

"When're you going to get your beauty shop hair?"

"Four o'clock tomorrow." I smiled. "Sit down, will you?"

"I got to go." He produced a gift-wrapped package from under his jacket. "I brought her a present."

"What is it?"

"It's straight stuff."

"What?"

He looked embarrassed. "It's a sterling silver salad fork." He explained about it. "I said to the lady at the jewelry store 'I want to get something for Miss Hannah Landrum who is getting married,' and the lady showed me this list as long as your arm and it showed how much each item cost and all I could get was the small-size fork." He stared at the gift with its commercial bridal bow.

"She will appreciate that, Roy."

"Don't give me that. She'll just toss it on the pile of loot. But that's what I want; I want to have something on the pile just the same as anybody else." The present was laid at the end of the table beside two forks like it.

"Are you doing all right?" I asked.

"I'm making it. Mom is staying off my back at least till fall. I'm going to get out of this buggy town for a while. I get a week off work, paid vacation. Not much you can do over Easter with the roads packed with the dentists from Houston in their air-stream campers. But I'm getting out."

"I wish I were."

"Where'd you want to go?"

"To a farm somewhere with pigs and cypress trees." My make-believe escape.

"What would *you* know how to do with pigs?"

Without even sitting down, Roy exited out the back door to spin his wheels down the gravel driveway past the yucca plants. He had it in his mind that things at my house had changed, even if I did not.

The major change is that Hannah will be under this roof no longer. My clearest memory of her as a child is not of my mothering her but of her mothering herself. It is as if I brought her home from the hospital, small, perfect girl with faint mat of hair, and at once she began to comfort herself for the world into which she had been plunged. When we were still with the CPA, there was Hannah, putting her doll on its bed, rocking and holding the rubber doll, patting the doll.

When we went back to Sally after Roger moved on, when it still seemed fitting to go home to Mother, at least as long as I could stand it, Hannah took to her grandmother's bedroom as if it were home.

Mother had one of those dolls with long gathered skirts, which, when turned upside down, was another doll with checked skirt and pigtails. Mother kept the doll for decora-

232

tion on the counterpane over her dust ruffle on their four-poster bed. There was the air about her room of a young girl's bedroom, as if Mother, each night when she went to sleep, dreamed herself back to her days as the high school queen.

Seeing Hannah sit on that ruffled bed and turn the doll back and forth while my mother brushed her hair into ringlets and talked to her about how when Grandmother was little she had long golden curls to her waist was what sent me looking for a job. I can see Hannah very very still, with the doll in her lap, and a blush on her cheeks as she allowed her crowning glory to be combed and brushed and twisted into curls about mother's finger, while Mother tended Hannah as Hannah had tended her dolls.

Later at Meg's there was Hannah passing up the rope swing in the back yard and the decrepit rose arbor where earlier tenants had tended garden, to play with an eye-less real china doll that had been Meg's mother's, decades before. We would find her lying with the doll against her cheek in the middle of my lumpy bed, fast asleep, and dreaming.

I must believe that my daughter will be where she has always wanted to be when she plumps the pillow on their double bed and tucks Eugene in each night, as she herself aches to be tucked.

"White has always been becoming to the Foster girls," Mother announces to the assembled. She beams like a sorority housemother at the wedding of a favorite.

After an hour of photographs in Dorothy's garden, of the Foster girls and their mother and the bride and her pink-gowned, pink-cheeked bridesmaids, we now wait on the organ chords in a small room off the sanctuary in the front of the church.

Hannah is a bride in tiers of gossamer veil which fall over her hair into a white curtain about her shoulders. She takes the breath away, looking like a novice being led from the cloister or a maiden from the final tower. Her pale hands hold fast to Dorothy's prayer book as Jenny Sue adjusts the folds of her dress in back.

"Dorothy, your wedding dress was the prettiest dress I have ever seen." Mother pulls on her youngest daughter's arm. "We went all the way to Dallas for it, remember? With all that appliquéd lace. Where is that dress now? Dorothy, do you know where we put your wedding dress?"

Mildred interrupts in a dull voice. "Mother, we don't need to know that now. This is Hannah's day."

Mother is not stopped. "It never hurts to have a little history thrown in, Millie. You were a lovely bride yourself in that heavy satin with the seed pearls on the bodice. When I think what your father paid then for that dress."

"It's in storage," Mildred tells her before she can ask. "It's in storage, Mother."

"Beverly, your hair looks like it had never been fixed." Mother turns her eyes on me and pushes at my waves to reinstate the paid-for look. We have each a band of satin on our heads to pass for hats; Mother, in addition, has her hairdo protected until the last minute by a chiffon scarf knotted under her chin. This one is lavender, to match the scoop-neck dress of the grandmother of the bride.

She has not been pleased with me since her arrival, which is an old pattern. If only I would take off my glasses for the photographs, and stand up straighter, and smile, if only I would look more presentable, less like Beverly.

The minute she walked in Dorothy's door she frowned, vexed to see me there, unchanged, still the middle girl.

"Well, aren't you even going to speak to your own mother?" she said.

"I said hello when you came in."

"Your father and I ought to get some thanks, I should think, for making that four-and-a-half-hour drive up here. It's your daughter we came to see, after all."

"Hannah wanted you to come."

"Are you saying it was no invitation of yours? Is that what you're saying? Girls, is that what Beverly's saying?"

"She's saying we're all here because we love Hannah," Mildred the mediator said patiently, Mildred who had driven all the way from the Valley with four children in the car.

"Your father deserves a special thank you for making that trip with his bad back."

But having her here is of course a reminder that there is no escape from the woman who bears you, just as Hannah must live out her life embarrassed by me.

Hannah bends her ear now to Dorothy, this aunt who also wed as an innocent sophomore, whose pink gown looks like faded rose petals pressed long ago in the pages of a book. As she hugs her niece, Dorothy whispers some special words of sisterhood, and Hannah smiles gratefully back at her.

This morning the CPA sent Hannah a dozen red roses that looked like an opening-night spray in the theatre. Some sick joke of his no doubt about "opening" night. When I gave birth to Hannah he sent word by one of the nurses that I was not to worry about my plumbing being out of order, that he had found a replacement for my parts. His idea of a joke.

But why remember that? Marriage does not have to be like that. Hannah will become a woman despite it; Ben and I will not inflict such scars again.

The room is warm with so many women and time stretches out. We who have been married stand clustered together in gloves and tight shoes, sharing a wish to believe, despite years of evidence to the contrary, that marriage can unite.

Bebe Lee, Cheryl, the other bridesmaids giggle nervously, full of longing for the bride's bouquet of white orchid and stephanotis. Jenny Sue, the maid of honor, produces the blue garter and slips it on Hannah's leg. She has happy tears in her eyes.

Here in the midst of envy and good wishes, in a room crowded with family and billowing with long, rustling skirts, I must say good-by to my daughter.

The organ prelude starts up; everyone but the wedding party needs to take a seat. Ben, the usher, waits outside the door for the mother of the bride.

"Beverly, why can't I remember your wedding dress? You were so peaked for a bride. But you wore Mildred's again, didn't you? Something borrowed." Mother clicks her tongue and unties her small square scarf.

I have rehearsed this. I have rehearsed this, wanting to make clear and audible before everyone that it is possible to please your mother. To tell Hannah that I know she has tried hard, and done her best, and been all she could be, and that is all we can expect of one another. Stepping slightly on her hem, disarraying slightly her white length of unstained veil, I press her to me closely and say the words only she will understand, "Honey, you are *enough* for me."

When the march begins there is a rustle as the small crowd turns to catch a glimpse of promise dressed in white. They strain to see the face of love behind her airy curtain. Only Eugene's mother does not move her plain face from watching her stalwart son make ready to receive a wife.

As Hannah walks in expectation down the narrow aisle love for her wells up in me as it should in the heart of a Hannah's mother under the eyes of God and in the company of a congregation of others.

When the minister asks, "Who gives this woman," I reach for Ben's hand and silently confess.

Epilogue

With my daughter gone, the house seems less crowded now, even the ghost of the dying woman has subsided to a faint rustle of papers. Ben and I love on the new queen-sized Serta; we read at our desks; we eat, as Hannah would wish it, on good dishes in the dining room. We have conjugal conversations about the drain spouts which are stopped with leaves, the crack in the plaster on the side of the house, the torn screen in the back door. Ben has made a room upstairs for all his spare books and gear long in storage. The small room, without its sewing machine, awaits a promised visit from Van, Jr., in August.

Ben and I tread carefully, making gestures of independence. For example last week with part of my lunch money I bought a *Scientific American* for an article on demography, and he came home with the same issue, which also had a study of linguistics in infant apes. It cost a dollar more to maintain separate lives, but we agreed that was a fair price to pay.

You think I am going to say marriage has provided me with the skinny black jersey dress in which to preside over faculty wine-tasting parties in the twelve-foot living room, but life does not resolve itself that way.

Rather, at the pine shelf which serves as a table, I have begun to make notes to myself somewhat like messages in a bottle, to mark our past and present days, against a future time when some new occupant hunts the house to see what clues remain. Better than a bedpan in the closet is the company town grown up in weeds in Sally, Texas, hot-water pipes in a strange hotel room, this dry stone fountain in the sun.

These notes give Foster definition as our planet crowds with new lives until we are set apart one from another only by the membrane of our skins, and as my own life grows intertwined with Ben and my sisters and the hair-dresser and Roy and the woman in the black shoes and Henry and the waitress and Eunice Fordyce and the great-aunt who smells of mothballs and Aunt Glad who wore no lipstick, and Clarice, and you.

It is important to leave behind in this yellow stucco house the image of one singular and separate life.